"Stop trying to get into my pants," Laine whispered

"Why?" Grayson meant the comment playfully, but he wanted her. It looked as if that wasn't going to happen right now, and he didn't understand why not.

"Because my pants are off-limits."

"From what you just told me about Men To Do, it sounds like open season."

"Not for you, Grayson. Been there, done you, not going there again."

"Okay. Message received and understood."

"Good." She let out a breath and grinned a sweet grin he was in no mood to return. "Now that's out of the way, are you hungry?"

She turned and reached up into a cabinet, causing her shirt to lift and expose the smooth skin of her midriff.

"Yeah, I'm hungry," Grayson muttered. Laine had no idea how hungry. But damn it, getting the meal he wanted was going to be much more of a challenge than he thought.

"You don't sound sure."

Dear Reader,

Here is my latest in the MEN TO DO series!

I deviated from the norm this time—my heroine Laine's
Men To Do adventures don't work out quite the way she
thinks they will, thanks to the reappearance of her first love,
Grayson Alexander.

The two of them try so hard not to fall back in love it's pathetic.
But of course they were never really out of it in the first place.
I read recently that some psychologists think you actually imprint
on your first love, which is why they theorize those men are so
tricky to remove from our hearts! Maybe you were lucky enough
to marry your first love? I'd love to hear the story (e-mail me
through www.IsabelSharpe.com).

And don't forget to check out the other MEN TO DO books
at our Web site, www.MenToDo.com.

I hope you enjoy Laine and Grayson's story.

Cheers,

Isabel Sharpe

Books by Isabel Sharpe

HARLEQUIN BLAZE
11—THE WILD SIDE
76—A TASTE OF FANTASY

HARLEQUIN DUETS
17—THE WAY WE WEREN'T
26—BEAUTY AND THE BET
32—A TRYST OF FATE
44—FOLLOW THAT BABY!
75—ONE FINE PREY
    TWO CATCH A FOX

TAKE ME TWICE

Isabel Sharpe

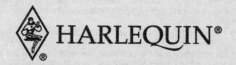

HARLEQUIN®

TORONTO • NEW YORK • LONDON
AMSTERDAM • PARIS • SYDNEY • HAMBURG
STOCKHOLM • ATHENS • TOKYO • MILAN • MADRID
PRAGUE • WARSAW • BUDAPEST • AUCKLAND

This book is dedicated to Namumi with great love.

ISBN 0-373-79130-5

TAKE ME TWICE

1

Hey, all. I am sitting here at my itsy-bitsy cubicle pretending to be typing up important memos, but it's my last day in this place (finally!) and all I'm really doing is watching the clock until my going-away party starts so everyone can come as an excuse to stop working, get free food and booze, and pretend they'll miss me and will keep in touch.

Wanting to spew coffee at the thought.

In any case, as you all know, the fact that I am leaving means, as I promised, that Men To Do season is wide open. I have an entire summer of unemployed bliss ahead of me before graduate school starts in September. During that time I plan to make some man or men extremely happy to be alive, and assume they will return the favor.

When September comes, I will start a part-time job, begin my studies and remember once again that men are more than penises mounted on thrusting devices.

For now, however, let the games begin.

Laine

"BYE, LAAAAAINE! We'll miss yooou, please keep in touch, okaaaaaay?"

"Oh, I *will*."

Not.

Laine returned the bare squeeze her soon-to-be ex-co-worker proffered, and nearly gagged on the way-too-familiar perfume stench. *Eau de Suffocation.* She sure as hell wouldn't miss that. This fact-checking job at *I am Woman* magazine was her fourth since graduating from Princeton eight years ago and she was done. Done! June first, and she was on her way to a summer of fun and relaxation before she started Columbia journalism school in the fall. Her first real break since…ever.

Ha! Take that, repressive slave-driving capitalist tools. She was history.

Her boss, Petunia Finkseed—whose real name was much less fun so why think of her that way—shook her hand gravely. "Thanks for the hard work and good luck, Laine. When you graduate, if you want to come back, please do. There's always a job for you here at *I am Woman*."

Laine grinned broadly, murmured thanks, and wondered just how high those pigs would have to fly before she'd think about coming back. Not that it had been a bad job, by any means. But she was free! *Free!* Free from the constant pressure, from the snarly office intrigue, from the barely veiled leers of the company V.P.

An entire summer stretched ahead of her; she'd

take Manhattan by storm, do all the things she'd wanted to since moving here after college but had never had time for. Sleeping late, reading the paper every day, taking long bubble baths, sight-seeing, irresponsibly late nights dancing during the week, trips to the beach, a solemn vow to avoid panty hose before 8:00 p.m. She wanted to take French, pottery, learn yoga, skydiving, tap dancing, cooking…

And…find a Man To Do. Or a couple of them.

She'd joined Eve's Apple, an online reading group, after her high school friend Samantha recommended it not only as a place to find fun and stimulating reads, but also as a good place for female companionship. Not long after, Laine had joined the smaller e-mail subset of the group, Men To Do Before Saying I Do. Their mission? To find unattached, sexy, thoroughly inappropriate males…and do them.

What could be more perfect? Call it an age-thirty midterm break. Then in September, graduate school at Columbia and the rest of her life would get started. She'd be on her way to becoming America's best reporter. Granted a few years ago she'd enrolled briefly in a master's English program at Boston University, and thought she was on her way to writing the Great American Novel; and granted after college she'd applied to medical school, but *this time* she was on her way. For real. She was pretty sure.

She grabbed her small box of personal items—pictures of her parents on their vacation at the Grand Canyon, her niece Carolyn on her first birthday, the scraggly air fern that, frankly, she couldn't tell was alive or dead, and the gold-plated bracelet her co-workers had chipped in and bought for her.

Outta here!

Her next-door cubicle prisoner, Fred, got a genuine hug and a promise of lunch sometime, and Laine fled.

Down the hall, down the elevator filled with tall, gorgeous women in black and men in dark suits, across the huge marble lobby filled with tall, gorgeous women in black and men in dark suits, and hot damn, out into the gritty dusty chaos of Times Square. Free! She wanted to hug the harassed mom with three cranky kids, she wanted to kiss the gorgeous blond guy across the street, she wanted to create a scene by skipping, no, frolicking, no, *gamboling* her way to the subway, kicking up her heels and crowing like Peter Pan.

Except, in Manhattan, no one would even blink.

She bounced down the 42nd Street subway stairs and pushed her way through the turnstile, following the commuting crowds the same way she always did. But instead of bleary-eyed, leaden, sheeplike, obedient herding, she practically danced onto the subway platform. *Hello, New Yorkers! Laine's here!*

She must be practically glowing. People would raise their heads and murmur when she walked by. Who was that woman with so much joy in her heart? What was her secret?

Instead she stepped in some just-chewed gum and spent a good three minutes trying to scrape the goo off the bottom of her chunky black heels.

No more black! The rest of the summer she'd avoid it like the plague. Except of course a killer black minidress on a hot date.

She filed onto the C-train, headed downtown and clutched her box of belongings, bumping against the other commuting bodies when the train swayed. She gazed at the ads along the top of the car to avoid gazing at other people, though she wished sometimes she could stare openly, like a child. Maybe she would do that sometime. People were so fascinating.

A body came a little too close behind her, pressed a little harder than the crush of commuters would make necessary. A pelvis planted firmly against her rear end. Ewwww. She grimaced and let her elbow make "accidental" forceful contact with the soft male belly behind her. There was a grunt, and the body moved away. City living could be so charming. But nothing could keep her down today. Nothing! Not even a gross grinder.

So what would she do tonight? Champagne? A soak in the tub? Maybe rent a nice romantic movie? Or maybe her roommate of six months, Monica, would want to go out, not that she ever did that anymore since she'd started dating Joe the Smotherer.

Just as well. Laine shouldn't go too wild too soon. Taking into consideration her grad school tuition and expenses, she'd saved barely enough to scrape through the summer without a salary, but finances would be tight if she went too crazy. She had a part-time job as a marketing writer with an architecture firm lined up this fall, but she'd really, really wanted the summer totally free.

The train arrived at Fourteenth Street. She got off and tossed a glare at the subway humper, who grinned back obscenely.

Ick.

Somehow she was always the target for the creepos. Maybe because she was tall, she hadn't a clue. Maybe she had been born with weirdo-magnet genes.

She charged up the stairs, enjoying the challenge to her body, and strode down Eighth Avenue to Jackson Square and toward her building on Horatio Street, mildly breathless. The sun was shining. Pigeons fluttered, shop windows sparkled, subways rumbled underground, taxis endangered pedestrians.

Everything was perfect.

She pushed through the revolving door to her building and waved at the tall, bushy-haired evening doorman. "Hey, Roger, what's going on?"

"More flowers." He bent slowly and pulled out a huge spring bouquet of tulips and irises from behind his station.

She shook her head, chuckling, and glanced at the card, not that she needed to. Ben. A guy she'd gone out with once or twice, a close friend of her cousin, Frank. Sweet man. Lovely man. Zero chemistry. At least on her end. And she wasn't sure on his, either; he acted more like a protective brother than a suitor. Maybe Frank had told him to watch out for her.

"This guy is nuts about you, huh?"

"Between you and me, Roger? He's just nuts."

Roger shrugged and fingered one of his enormous ears. "He's sure trying hard."

"He loves sending flowers, I guess. You want this one for Betty?"

Roger's red, lined face broke into a smile that transformed him from a sour, craggy Scrooge to an indicator of the handsome man he must have been thirty years ago before, she suspected, a love affair with the bottle had begun. "Betty thinks *I've* gone nuts. But she sure appreciates it."

"They're yours. He won't let me send them back, refuses to stop, and the bouquet upstairs is still plenty fresh."

She waved to acknowledge his thanks, got her mail

from the back room and took the elevator to the eighth floor.

Friday evening, sprung free from employment, the city waited, the summer was at her feet.

She put her key in the lock of apartment 8-C, pushed open the door and stopped. Monica was sobbing over an open suitcase on the living room couch, clothes strewn all around it.

"Monica!" Laine rushed into the room, forgetting to hold the door, which slammed behind her, sounding like doom. "What's going on?"

"He…he…he…"

Laine waited while the word surfed out on sobs. "Joe?"

She nodded. "He…he…he…"

"Oh no." Laine moved forward and put her hand on Monica's shoulder. Whatever he…he…he had done, it didn't sound good. And from what she'd seen of Joe—cocky, brash, overbearing, big-nosed, obnoxious—she was only surprised it had taken this long.

"Dumped you?"

"Yes." The word came out on a wail of anguish.

"So—" Laine gestured around "—why are you packing?"

"I'm going home."

Laine turned her shaking roommate around by the shoulders, melting in sympathy. She'd been exactly where Monica was four months ago, with Brad—a stunning, charming, self-absorbed, cheating sleazebag. "I totally understand. A little TLC from your parents is just what you need."

"No. You don't understand." Monica pulled back and wiped her blue eyes, smudging her already smudged mascara into bigger raccoon circles. "I'm not visiting. I'm moving."

Laine's melting sympathy froze temporarily. "Moving?"

Monica nodded and fished inside the pocket of her black stretch jeans, most likely for a tissue.

Laine blew out a breath, trying very hard to concentrate on her latest roommate's emotional needs. No way could she afford the rent on this place by herself all summer with no salary.

But this wasn't about her. And even pushing aside her selfish concerns, she genuinely thought Monica was making a mistake. No man was worth running back to Iowa. Not after Monica had worked so hard to make her dream of living in the Big Apple come true.

"You can't let him win like that." Laine gestured impatiently. "You can't toss aside your independence and career and dream just because one big, butthead male hurt you. You're made of sterner stuff than that."

"That's not all." She sniffed and tried another pocket.

"Oh." Laine went for the box of Kleenex, half feeling as though she might need one herself. "Well, what else?"

"Mr. Antworth made another pass at me this afternoon, and I quit." She grabbed a tissue and blew her nose, then went back to her misery-impaired packing.

Laine's eyes narrowed. "Okay, you're right. This was a seriously awful day. Mr. Antworth should have a dick-ectomy. But you can press charges. You can fight to get your job back and bring him down. Or get another job. You don't have to—''

''And my mom's back in rehab.''

Laine took two steps west until the back of her knees hit her couch. She sat. Opened her mouth. Closed it. Opened it again. ''Oh my God, Monica.''

Monica closed her suitcase and zipped it. ''I'm going home. My dad needs me, and I need to get out of here.''

''Oh, God, yes. Okay, yes. Is there anything I can do?''

''I'm really sorry to leave you like this.'' Monica started crying again. ''I know you wanted to take the summer off.''

''No! No.'' Laine waved her concerns away. ''I'll be fine. It's June, there must be tons of people looking for a place to live. It's fine. Don't worry about me. You just take care of yourself.''

''Thanks.'' Monica lugged her suitcase off the couch. ''I better go.''

''Now?'' Laine blinked at her stupidly. ''You're leaving now?''

''My plane leaves at nine tonight. I'll come back for the rest of my stuff or send for it or…something. I just can't deal with it now.''

''Oh. Okay.'' Laine nodded even more stupidly. Her brain was barely taking this in. Instinct told her Monica was doing this all wrong, that making a major life change should be done in a calmer, more rational mindset than she was in today.

One more look at the confused misery in her roomie's eyes and the solution hit. ''Leave the stuff here. I'll find someone temporary to see me through for a while. Take a couple of weeks at home, or a month, or two, and see how you feel. If you change your mind the place is still yours. Okay?''

Monica's face crumpled in gratitude. "Thank you. Thank you so much. Yes, okay. I just need to get out of here now.''

Laine hugged her. "I understand. I really do. The place will be waiting. You take your time and sort things out.''

"Thanks for everything." Monica stepped back and wiped at her face with the by-now-soggy tissue, rapidly turning gray with a little help from Maybelline. "Say goodbye to Gentle Ben for me. I'll miss all the flowers.''

"I'll have every other bouquet forwarded." Laine laughed unsteadily. "Stay in touch. You know the number.''

"I will, I will." Monica sniffed once more and wheeled her suitcase out of the apartment. The door slammed behind her. Laine stared at it.

"She'll be back, won't she?''

The door didn't answer. The apartment seemed eerily silent.

Laine crossed her arms over her chest, wandered into the bathroom and turned on the water to wash her workday makeup off. Poor Monica. Hit from every direction at once.

The cold water faucet squeaked on its way to off. Laine grabbed her pink towel and held it to her dripping face. Monica had been the best roommate she'd found, the friend of a friend of a friend. They fit perfectly. Similar habits, tastes, schedules, temperaments. How likely was it she could find someone like that again?

Not very.

How likely was it that she could find someone like that again *immediately*, who would be willing to be booted out on a moment's notice if Monica decided to come back?

Even less.

She pulled the towel down and looked at her pink-scrubbed face in the mirror, pulled the scrunchy off her ponytail and let her hair dissolve into a blunt, shoulder-length, too-straight mane around her face. For the past six months Laine had looked forward to this summer, free from work, free from relationships, looked forward to this free-from-responsibilities blast-off period for a new rewarding chapter of her life.

Now, unless she could find an instant miracle roommate, that freedom, that cherished vision of a playtime summer all her own wasn't going to happen.

GRAYSON ALEXANDER'S clock radio went off— 6:00 a.m. He groaned and opened his eyes reluctantly. Extremely reluctantly. Because before National Public Radio news had come on with a story about Wisconsin dairy farmers, he'd been nestled between two of the most fabulous legs he'd ever come across in all his thirty-two years. Legs that knew exactly what they were doing. It had been years since they'd been wrapped around him, but he'd never forget them. And if his subconscious had anything to do with it, he'd never stop wishing to be back between them.

He reached out, thumped the snooze button on top of his clock radio and buried his head back in his pillow, trying to recapture the vivid clarity of the dream. He could still almost smell her, that incredible scent she wore, could almost feel the softness of her skin. The dreams he had about Laine were totally different from the dreams he had about anything or anyone else. They were so real he always woke up—hard as granite, yes—but also feeling as if there was something he should do, as if the dreams brought some message he shouldn't—and generally couldn't—ignore.

Usually he called Judy, his and Laine's friend from college. He'd ask how things were, chat uncomfortably for a while, knowing he wasn't fooling her a bit by pretending interest in her life, and eventually he'd ask what Laine was up to. Was she happy? Was she thriving? And, damn it, always that question that could never come out sounding casual and disinterested no matter how hard he tried—was she seeing anyone? Invariably she was, though rarely the same guy as the last time he and Judy had spoken.

The weird thing was, he always seemed to have these dreams when her life had changed in some way—another job didn't work out, another man bit the dust—which freaked him right out. Purportedly, he didn't buy into all that mystical collective unconscious stuff. Nor did he believe he and Laine had some special link, though God knew he'd never come close to feeling what he did for her with anyone else. But he sure as hell couldn't explain this. Worse, rather than being satisfied having found out what Laine was up to, he'd hang up from the calls feeling frustrated and angry, and never able to put his finger on why.

Then a few months or a year down the road, he'd dream another dream, and do the entire stupid-assed routine again. Doubtless this morning, after his workout and before he started his calls, he'd be on the phone to Judy again.

He let out a groan and bunched the pillow around his ears, then sat up and shot both hands through his hair. Fine. He still thought about her once in a while. He still wanted her. Didn't mean his whole life revolved around her. He'd work out, shower, call Judy and get the whole thing out of his system.

For now.

He pulled on his running shoes, shorts and a T-shirt, went down the hardwood stairs to his large, sunny kitchen and poured himself a glass of orange juice. A little sugar in his system to get him through his run. Then out the front door, greeting the morning with a huge breath, stretches in his driveway and a two-mile trip through Princeton's peaceful residential neighborhoods, particularly gorgeous in the spring when homeowners outdid each other with floral splendor, and dogwoods and magnolias blossomed in the woods and along the streets.

Back home on Knoll Drive, he went into his basement for extra punishment with his weight machines. He and Laine used to work out together. Sometimes he'd do her girly aerobic tapes, which he'd never admit busted his ass, and sometimes she'd come with him jogging. Those legs of hers could run forever. Once in a while he'd drop behind her deliberately to enjoy the sight—her ponytail bouncing, feet pounding, arms pumping an easy rhythm. They'd shared a passion for working their bodies to the limit, in bed and out.

The barbell clanged back onto his weight rack. Damn it all to hell.

He wiped off with a towel and stomped upstairs in disgust. They'd broken up because of his immature collegiate stupidity twelve years ago, thinking he could have his Laine and eat Joanne, too. He was still suffering for it, even though they'd managed to stay friends after the worst blew over. In fact, they'd seen each other off and on for the next seven years while they'd both lived in New York, before he moved to Chicago and they'd lost touch. Or rather, he'd tried to block her out.

Fat chance.

He took the second set of stairs two at a time and ran into the bathroom, shed his clothes, turned the stream full-blast and hot. Scrubbed furiously at his skin and hair, then stood, eyes closed, letting the water flow over him, then letting the memories do the same. He and Laine loved sex in the shower. She'd slide her slippery, soapy body over him, down to her knees, take him in her mouth and blow his mind. She'd tip her head up, his cock still between her lips, and give him that look of sensual mischief that said, *You are so in my power, little boy.* He'd reach for her and push her against the cracked yellowing tile in his crappy New York apartment and show her who was really in control.

God, they'd had fun. Sure, sex with other women since then had been fun, too. But nothing like the wild, playful passion with Laine. Even after their initial breakup, after the anger and bitterness and pain had blown over and they'd managed to be friends again, getting together invariably involved sex. Plenty of it. All incredible.

Grayson yanked off the shower, grabbed his towel and dragged it roughly over his body. Better get going. Time spent in useless mooning was wasted. He wasn't even going to call Judy today or any other day to see what was up with Laine. Now that he was back east, the temptation to start things up again would drive him nuts. He hadn't seen her in five years, not since he'd moved to Chicago. What was done was done.

He pulled on shorts and a cotton shirt and prepared for his morning commute to his office—a converted bedroom on the second floor. Given his and Chuck's start-up company's cramped and only semiprivate office space at 1841 Broadway, opting to call from home had been a no-brainer.

He sat at his desk and brought up the week's schedule on his monitor. Meetings in the city nearly every day this week, which meant he'd get into the office fairly regularly, but spend too many back-and-forth hours on NJ Transit trains. Damn shame he couldn't afford a studio for overnights. But with the price of real estate in N.Y., a midtown, one-room apartment would set him back more than his entire three-bedroom house here. And Princeton wasn't exactly bargainsville.

He opened his e-mail program, scanned the messages, deleted ads promising him a larger penis or a chance to earn thousands at home.

Good. Carson Industries wanted a bid for their Web site; he'd send an e-mail to Chuck to let him know. And he'd managed to sell Granger Healthcare on the idea of redesigning theirs; they wanted a bid, too. Excellent. Other than that, more calls to make, trying to put Jameson Productions on the map in the Web design business. They'd done very well so far—he'd brought in enough jobs that they'd had to hire a second programmer, and Chuck had finally gotten his dearest wish—an assistant to spare him paperwork.

So it looked as though he'd be on the phone most of the day. Just not to Judy.

He picked up the receiver, made a call to Ralph Scannell, V.P. of Marketing at Office Mart, who was not Judy and who knew nothing about Laine. Ralph wasn't interested in a new Web site or any other promotional material. Grayson shrugged. Rejection was part of the job. He made another call, strangely enough also not to Judy. Managed to chat with the office manager, but was stalled trying to get someone higher up in marketing. Three more calls, then three more, none of them to the woman known as Judy or anyone who could possibly tell him anything about his sexy ex-girlfriend Laine Blackwell.

In fact, he was going to sit here, with his butt parked in his overpriced ergonomically correct chair and not call Judy all damn morning long.

2

"YOU'LL NEVER GUESS who called me."

Laine glanced up from her menu at Clark's Diner, her and her oldest friend Judy's regular Saturday lunch spot. She had a pretty good idea. The same person it always was when Judy said, "You'll never guess who called me."

"Who?"

Judy leaned forward, one dark brow lifted, brown eyes sparkling behind her narrow, aqua-framed glasses. "Grayson Alexander."

"No kidding." Laine did a quick internal scan of her emotions, noting with triumph that she wasn't feeling even a hint of that crazy thrill his name used to provoke in her without fail. Nothing but friendly, affectionate warmth. "What's he up to?"

"The usual." Judy sat back, watching Laine entirely too carefully, so Laine continued to explore the menu she knew practically by heart. She wasn't in the mood to be psychoanalyzed. She'd been trying to find a roommate for an entire week, in fact had interviewed her sixth candidate this morning. A woman named Shadow, who hoped it would be okay if she burned incense every day. Oh, and her pet rat would be welcome, wouldn't he? Worse, Shadow had been the most promising candidate.

"He and Chuck Gartner—do you remember him?

He was a year older than us at Princeton. Charming geek, about twenty feet tall..."

"Yes, I remember."

"He and Chuck are making a go of their interactive media business. They have an office on Broadway by the park. And Grayson bought a house in Princeton on Knoll Drive."

Laine nodded. "Sounds like he's doing well."

"I know. Huge sigh." Judy patted her ample chest. "He still makes my heart go pitter-pat. Killer looks, perfect body and enough charm to sink the *Titanic*. Not that he'd look at a lonely, overweight doormat like me."

"Oh, will you stop." Laine glared and held up a finger. "One, you are not overweight and—"

"Ahem." Judy raised her hand to interrupt. "I weigh what you do and I'm a foot shorter."

"Eight inches. And I'm a beanpole. Two—" she held up a second finger "—you're only lonely because you don't get out there and find people to—"

"So shoot me, I'm shy."

"Three, you—hey!" Laine let her hand smack down on the table. "Why don't you find a Man To Do, too?"

Judy scrunched up her face incredulously. "Me? Are you kidding? I walk into a bar, men run out screaming."

Laine rolled her eyes. "Utter crap. What about... whatshisname? At that bar we went to the night you—"

"Roy?" Judy pointed to her chest. "He was just into boobs."

"Well...there's a start. I mean they're part of you."

Judy let out a snort of laughter and shook her head. "Men To Do is not for me. I can't screw a guy for the hell of it. I have sex once, I want to wash his socks for all eternity. It's just who I am."

"Nonsense. I used to be that way, too, but I evolved. You can, too."

"Evolved?" Judy scoffed. "You mean you got massively hurt by Grayson and are scared to try again."

"No." The casual denial came out not so very casually and a strange, angry feeling invaded her stomach. "You're always romanticizing our relationship. I was twenty. He was my first love. At that age, I thought if you fell in love, that was that, you had forever all sewn up."

"It can be that way."

Laine put down her menu and pressed tense fingers to her temples. "Trust me, I know. I hear it every time I go home. That's how it was with my mom forty years ago and my sister ten years ago and what's the matter with me that I can't hang on to a man? I say they were just plain lucky meeting Mr. Right the first time. Nothing is 'forever' for sure. Not marriage, not career, not anything."

Judy waved her off dismissively. "Gloom and doom."

"It's not all gloom. Look at all the stuff I've done in my life. I've had four jobs, dated six men, tried two different grad school programs and am headed for a third, met tons of people—I've had a blast. I've really lived, unlike my parents and sister who've done the exact same thing every day of their lives since birth. If I'd married Grayson I'd probably be at home now in the same house I'd lived in forever, in the same bathrobe and slippers I'd had forever, trying to keep track of about a hundred children.'' She shuddered. ''Now *that* is gloomy.''

''I don't know.'' Judy sighed and fingered the necklace of colored-glass beads at her throat. ''Sounds pretty great to me.''

''Instead.'' Laine picked up her water glass and toasted her friend. ''Instead, I'm totally free and about to embark on my next great adventure.''

''Right.'' Judy's cynical eyebrow crept up the left side of her forehead, even as she hoisted her water glass and clinked with Laine. ''He's not seeing anyone, you know.''

''Who?'' She knew damn well who. She just didn't want to admit that he'd stayed in her mind even this long.

''Grayson.''

''And?''

''Neither are you.''

''And neither are *you,* Ms. I'll-always-love-Grayson. Why don't *you* try to go out with him?''

''Ohhhh, no. Oh, no. Ohhhh, nononono.'' Judy turned a lovely shade of pink to match her cotton sweater. ''Not me. This guy will always belong to you.''

Laine threw up her hands in surrender. ''How can you think that? You were there for the entire fiasco in college. We weren't meant to be. What's the point of drumming all that up again?''

''Let's just say that as much as it would make my life, I am under no illusion that he wants to know how *I* am when he calls. He always mumbles for a while then gets to the real point—'How is Laine doing?' ''

"So?" Laine picked up her menu. She was not getting into this. She was hungry and it would only make her cranky. Grayson was ancient history, and happily so. It had taken her years and years and years to get over him, her first real love; she wasn't anxious to stir that up again. "He just wants to know how I am."

"Nope. It's more than that. He gets all awkward and choky-sounding when he asks."

"Hair ball?" She moved from Salads to Sandwiches. Nothing appealed.

"Laine."

"Maybe he's eating." Burgers, no. Chili, no.

Judy made a sound that demonstrated in no uncertain terms what she thought of that possibility. "I told him you were looking for a roommate."

"Uh-huh." Laine's eyes zeroed in on her usual lunch order. Okay, so she always had it, but today was a comfort food kind of day and the chicken noodle soup at Clark's was delicious, rich and full of big pieces of chicken.

"He said he was interested."

Laine's head jerked up. "Interested?"

Judy crossed her arms over her chest, looking like the winner of a smug contest. "I thought that might grab your attention."

"Interested in what, interested?"

"Interested in being your roommate, interested."

Laine closed her menu. Her body and brain seemed to be on hold until they decided how to react to that one. "I thought you said he had a house in Princeton."

"He does. But he has appointments in the city, and

it would be easier for him not to have to commute back and forth on the train.''

''Oh.'' Still no reaction. She wasn't sure if that was good or not.

''He's willing to cough up half your rent and only stay there when he needs to.''

''Oh.''

Judy beckoned as if she were trying to coax words out of Laine's mouth. ''So?''

Laine stared at her friend, no doubt looking utterly blank. She hadn't a clue what to think. Or feel. Grayson Alexander wanted to be her roommate. Grayson Alexander. Wanted to be her roommate. Her roommate. Gray—

''So, what do you say?'' Judy was leaning forward again, scheming eyes alight.

''I don't know.'' Laine glanced around the diner as if the other customers might be able to step in to tell her what to say. ''I guess it sounds…ideal.''

''You don't sound like you guess it sounds ideal.''

''No. It does. It sounds ideal. I guess.''

''Of course it sounds ideal. Because it *is* ideal.'' Judy pounded her small fist on the table. ''It's totally ideal. You guys are friends, you know him, you can trust him not to steal from you or have any weird habits or friends. No risk. And he won't even be there most of the time. I'm telling you, it's perfect.''

''Well.'' She nodded seriously. ''I guess it is.''

''It's more than perfect.'' Judy gestured into the air, then clasped her hands. ''It's fate.''

Laine narrowed her eyes. ''Okay, let's not get carried away.''

''But you'll say yes?''

She shrugged, feeling off balance and totally unused to the feeling. It was pretty amazing timing that Grayson had called Judy just when Laine was looking for someone. And it did seem the perfect solution. The obvious choice.

It's just that this little tiny voice inside her was sounding a warning. Perfect solutions and obvious choices had this way of turning on her. Jobs turned out to be deadening, men turned out to be wrong for her, graduate programs turned out not to be her calling.

But the voice wasn't really loud enough for her to hear the details of what it thought was so wrong, and the overwhelming practicality of the solution was pretty compelling. In one stroke she could secure her playtime summer, save herself from having to live with a stranger and, as it turned out, she'd have the place to herself most of the time anyway.

Laine looked at the anxious face across the table and grinned. Not to mention Ms. Puppy Love would have easy drooling access. How could she say no? "Well, I mean, if he calls and asks and it all seems…well, yeah."

"Hurray!" Judy threw up her hands and nearly punched the waitress who had finally arrived.

Laine smiled wanly and placed her order for the chicken soup. Definitely a comfort food day. She hadn't seen Grayson in years. Five to be exact. She heard news of him now and then, maybe a couple of times a year if that, through Judy. After the initial nasty breakup, when she'd caught him with his fingers in another cookie jar, they'd managed to be friends for years, though admittedly they'd always seemed to stretch the boundaries of "friendship" to include sex. Lots of sex. Fabulous sex. Then he'd moved to Chicago and that was that. An unspoken agreement that it was time to move on. Now he was back in the area and she'd not only see him, she'd share intimate living space with him.

Okay. She could do that. She was way over him. They were friends. Buddies. Right?

"You okay?"

Laine blinked across the table to find Judy looking at her over the tops of her funky glasses with concern. A giddy bubble of laughter swelled in Laine's chest. Her worries were ridiculous. Grayson was an old friend—granted, a friend she'd wanted to marry at one point, but that was years and years and years ago. They'd both moved on and she was a different person now. Rooming together was merely a practical arrangement to get them through the summer. She'd be out most of the time in pursuit of her adventures and her Man To Do and he'd be into whatever or whoever he was into.

Of course she was okay.

"Yes. Yes. I'm fine. I'm totally fine. I'm more than fine." She laughed and handed her menu to the waitress. "In fact, thanks to Grayson, this is once again going to be the best summer of my life."

From: Angie Keller
Sent: Sunday
To: Laine Blackwell; Kathy Baker
Subject: Men To Do

Why, honey chile, welcome to paradise! I am so glad you will be joining us! Me, I found a Man To Do only last night and my, my, my, I am feeling quite Queenly today. He was extremely manly and possessed an oh-so-talented tongue. My mama would have fainted dead away if she knew how I carried on. But I say God gave me this body to use, and I'm doing it.

Have fun!
God bless,
Angie

From: Kathy Baker
Sent: Sunday
To: Laine Blackwell; Angie Keller
Subject: Way To Go!

Wow, Laine, you are ready to roll! And okay, you have given me courage, I really need to do this (one of these days). I just don't know where to meet men! The ones online here in Milwaukee seem so not my type—okay, maybe I overanalyze—but I can't get excited about any of them just from a squinty little picture. Guys, a little tip: it is so not enticing to see half an arm around your neck from where you cut your last girlfriend out of the photo.

I wish I had Harlot Angie's balls and could walk into a bar and just pick a guy out.

Anyway, congrats on your free summer and keep us posted!!
'Bye,
Kathy

GRAYSON HUNG UP the phone in total unabashed triumph. He was the salesman of all salesmen. The *über*-salesman. He'd just taken a call from a guy named Bob, who was trying to sell *him* some sales-training course. In the space of a half hour, Grayson had carefully and skillfully turned the conversation around, found out Bob's company needed a new Web site, and secured a sales appointment for Jameson Productions, his own damn company.

He chuckled, reveling in that moment of rare beauty when Bob the Salesman Trainer had realized what was happening to his high-pressure call.

Hey, you're selling me.

Grayson stretched one side of his body, then the other and leaned back in his chair, hands clasped behind his head.

Listen. That was all you had to do. Listen and ask questions. People would always tell you what you needed to know to get in. Too many salesmen did the professional equivalent of trying to carve a delicate wooden figurine with an ax. The good citizens of this country were axed every day with information, requests, advertisements, news, bothered at home by telemarketers, overwhelmed with options. To make a difference, all you had to do was shut up and listen. Use your tiniest chisel and, bit by bit, make that figurine emerge.

In six months Grayson had grown his and Chuck's company to where they were on target for a half-million in annual business. And he was only just starting. What he needed now was one plum, one ripe, gorgeous, enormous company with ongoing needs for Jameson's Web design and interactive media offerings.

It was out there. He just needed to find it. Having Laine's place to stay in would give him more time in the city, more time for appointments, more time to see Chuck and the programmers for face-to-face consulting on projects, and less time commuting.

He pushed back against the chair, making its upholstered metallic innards creak. Not that less time sitting on trains was the only reason he'd jumped at the idea. He called Judy because he was being ridiculous, acting as if sitting home avoiding Laine was some show of strength. He wanted to see her again. Wanted to find out why she still invaded his dreams. And yeah, he wanted to do some other things that he better not admit, because it wasn't very gentlemanly of him to be thinking of her that way after five years, before he'd even been able to talk to her again.

Grayson picked up the phone and dialed her number, his heart still racing from his morning run, coffee and the thrill of success securing another appointment. He'd been about to call Laine when this bozo Bob had called him. Now he couldn't wait to hear her voice.

"Hello?"

She was out of breath. A grin spread over his face. Hot damn. He couldn't help it. She sounded so good.

"You working out or something more fun?"

"Grayson?"

The sound of his name from her mouth made him smile harder. "How are you, Laine?"

"Grayson! I'm fine, how the hell are *you?* Judy said you'd call. God, it's been five years."

"I know. But I thought of you every one of them."

She gave a familiar snort of laughter. "How sweet."

"Yeah, well…" He put his feet up on his desk. "That's me."

"Though I noticed when you picked up the phone, you always called Judy."

He went to cross his ankles and both feet slipped off the desk, nearly toppling him out of his chair. "Hmm…yeah, well…Judy is…she's…Judy is Judy."

"And Laine is Laine?"

"And never the twain, yeah."

He grinned, picturing her talking to him on the phone—tall, slender, dark hair, blue eyes, flushed from working out. The kind of woman who drew men's stares everywhere she went, all the more because she was so unconscious of how stunning she was.

"So now after five years, five thoughts of me and phone calls to Judy-who-is-Judy instead of Laine-who-is-Laine, you suddenly want to move in with me?"

"Something like that."

"Well, there's a switch."

He left the barb alone. "Work with me here, Laine."

"I don't know…" She responded to his tease with mock hesitancy. "I'm not much of a worker these days."

"Then play with me?"

"Play with yourself."

He burst out laughing. Bam! Walked right into that one. You couldn't get much past Laine Blackwell. "Okay, okay. Yes, I want to move in with you. A few nights a week when I have appointments in the city."

"Why?"

"Didn't Judy tell you?"

"Forget Judy. Tell Laine-who-is-Laine."

"Okay, Laine-who-is-Laine. Having an apartment in the city will help me professionally."

"Ah." She blew out a sigh. "So you finally admit you need professional help."

He couldn't stop grinning. He suddenly missed her fiercely, as if all the years they'd been apart had hit him retroactively. "That's right."

"This is good. You must have come a long way."

"You *know* I can come a long way."

Her turn to laugh, that big, loud, honest belly laugh she released when something really struck her. He was pumped by the sound, even higher than he'd been. And turned on, totally jazzed by their sparring. He couldn't wait to see her. And yeah, there were still one or two of those ungentlemanly thoughts on his mind. In fact there were lots of them. Who was he kidding? He was no gentleman when it came to Laine. Though only once had he stooped to being an outright jerk, an episode he still wished he could go back in time and erase.

"Are you going to let me in, Laine?"

"Into my apartment."

"Of course? What else would I mean?" He grinned, waiting, rubbing his thumb along his chin.

"Nothing." She took a deep breath and let it out.

His grin faded. "Is there a problem?"

"No. No. There's not a problem."

He cocked his head. There was a problem. He hoped to hell she was merely rediscovering her need to be naked under him. "Why the hesitation?"

"It's fine. You can stay here when you need to. It will be fine."

"You don't sound sure."

"I'm sure."

She wasn't sure. Maybe he'd gone too far. "You understand that I'm doing this because of my job."

"Oh, of course. Of course. I understand that."

Was she relieved? Sorry? Embarrassed? He couldn't tell without seeing her face. "Because given our history, I didn't want you to think I was only trying to get into your pants again."

Which was true. He wasn't *only* trying to get into her pants. He did need a base in Manhattan.

"Oh, no. I didn't think that at all. Honest, Grayson."

He frowned. Where was the zinging comeback? She sounded utterly sincere. It must have occurred to her they could get back together for some fun. Judy had said she wasn't involved with anyone. Two consenting adults with a history of explosive chemistry. In the same apartment. All night long. Didn't take much imagination to keep the scenario heating up.

But then she'd always been pretty naive about his basely motivated gender. For a second he nearly felt ashamed of himself, but then shame was a useless emotion and it wasn't as if he was planning to force her. He knew he could make her want him, even after this many years. Whatever that sexual TNT was between them, he had a feeling it would never go away. He'd bet his company they'd be in the sack together within a week.

And Grayson Alexander never made bets he could lose.

3

From: Laine Blackwell
Sent: Monday
To: Angie Keller; Kathy Baker
Subject: Men To Do and (ack!) Old Boyfriend Returns

First things first, I've decided that hanging out in bars is not going to get me my Man To Do. Too iffy, too expensive, too dangerous. And I've either met or dated all my friends' available male friends, so no point going that route. Therefore (drumroll and trumpet flourish), I've been cruising NYdates.com. Can't say for sure I won't find any weirdos there, but I figure if I can thumbs-up pictures that attract me and thumbs-down men who can't put two sentences together (or punctuate, what is up with that?), then I'm ahead of the game.

And, well, *what* do you know, I have found a few possibles, one in particular, Antonio, a dark and *very* sexy-looking Italian (attached is the link to his profile and photo), who fits my height and punctuation requirements and who sounds totally full of himself, which I'm thinking would classify him as…let's say…the Vain Foreigner. I've e-mailed him, so we'll see what happens.

Woohoo! This summer is going to be so incredible! I've signed up for a yoga class and a cooking class, and I found this skydiving company in N.J. and a tap-dancing class and I'm going to take a French class, too, and I'm so into this!

Okay, I better go. In a very short while, Grayson shows up. I'm excited about seeing him and, okay, nervous and not really sure what it will be like. I mean we were sort of obsessed with each other for a lot of years even after we broke up. It took him moving to Chicago to finally get him out of my head, not to mention my bed. But he's definitely out and will stay out of both! So we'll see.

'Bye!

Laine

P.S. Of course I'll give the full report if my Vain Foreigner writes back.

GRAYSON STRODE DOWN the dark, stuffy, narrow eighth-floor hallway of Laine's apartment building, carrying his overnight bag, briefcase and laptop, and clutching the enormous bouquet Roger the doorman had asked him to bring up. Apparently some guy named Ben was sending Laine flowers on a regular basis. Grayson did not like the sound of that, not that he had a claim on her anymore. Not yet at least.

Eight-K, 8-L… He reached 8-M before his brain kicked in that he was going the wrong way to get to 8-C. He let out a groan and turned around, wanting to wipe away perspiration at his temple, but too impatient to drop everything to take care of it.

What a day. Disaster meeting at Borg Engineering, a cancellation at ETJ Hutchins, which they hadn't bothered to mention until he'd shown up, and now he found the idea of this guy sending Laine flowers damned irritating. A lot of money to be spending on a woman who wasn't interested if what Roger said was true. Grayson wasn't so sure. A guy would have to be nuts to invest that kind of money and energy into anything but a sure lay.

No point wasting time sniveling about it. Grayson was going to be spending time with her—intimate, everyday-living time. If this guy wanted her, he was going to have to do a lot better than dialing his florist.

Eight-A, 8-B and bingo, 8-C. He grinned at the number and jabbed the buzzer—four short, one long, two short, one long—Morse code for S-E-X, a silly game they'd started in college. It was going to be so good to see her. He wouldn't be surprised if the sight of her induced the rush it always had, even when he saw her every day.

The door swung open and she stood there smiling. Yeah, the same rush hit him, maybe twice as hard for all the years he'd been without her.

"Laine." He bent to ditch his laptop, overnight bag and briefcase, and gathered her in for a one-armed hug, inhaling her scent, wishing he could drop the damn vase to hold her the way he wanted. She always managed to smell as if she'd just come home from a day in a field of wildflowers. Total aphrodisiac.

He released her only far enough to bring her face into focus. Five years older, but only more beautiful. Blue eyes shining under straight, dark hair, perfect skin—to hell with getting reacquainted; he wanted to drag her off to his cave right this second. "It's much too good to see you."

She pulled away, laughing and flushed, and took the flowers he handed her. Immediately he missed her warmth and energy and wanted them back.

"Wow, are these from you, Grayson?" She lifted the vase, teasing already. She knew the odds of him thinking to buy her flowers were about one in several hundred million.

"Aren't they always?"

"Um, no?"

"Some guy named Ben apparently makes this a habit." He watched her closely. "Friend of yours?"

"Not really." She darted a glance down and back. "A friend of my cousin's. He's just—"

"Trying to get in your pants? Or thanking you for having been there." He registered the sharp edge in his voice at the same time she did and wasn't sure which of them was more surprised. Down, boy. Stay cool.

"Oh, for—" She threw up her free hand in a typical Laine gesture of exasperation. "Still thinking with your other head, I see."

"It's my favorite." He shrugged, all innocence.

She grinned unwillingly. "Ben's harmless. Zero interest on my part, I even told him so. Right now he's just my self-appointed protector and florist."

"You told him you weren't interested, and he's still sending you flowers?"

She nodded and inhaled rapturously over the blooms. "He's a very sweet man."

"No one's *that* sweet."

"Hmm." She lifted her eyebrows. "Not that I

would expect *you* to know anything about the concept, but apparently some men are.''

''Ha!'' He grinned and put his hands on his hips, studying her, the tension of the day falling away, the energy she'd always been able to light in him strong as ever. ''It's damn good to see you, Laine.''

''You, too, Grayson.'' Her gaze lingered and softened. ''You look great.''

''Not as great as you.'' He meant it. She was still his every fantasy of woman—city sexiness and sophistication layered over this elusive country-fresh thing she had going. His very first glance at her clingy midthigh skirt and knit sleeveless top told him her body was still strong and lean. And he knew what she could do with every square inch of it.

But he supposed suggesting they retire immediately to her bedroom for some naked gymnastics would be pushing it.

''How are your folks?'' He reached to her forehead to brush aside hair that wasn't out of place.

''Fine. Terrific. Whatever.'' She lifted her arm, let it drop down against her thigh. ''I've lived here for eight years—Mom still tells me I better come home where I belong and did I know Geoffrey Wrango was divorced and he's always asking after me, and my sister is expecting her gazillionth child next month and aren't I worried about getting too old? Because I can have a career anytime, but the longer I wait the greater my chances of having a kid with Down's or not conceiving at all, plus at my age the good men are going fast, and by the way my father isn't going to last forever and how hard could it be to jump on a plane back to Ohio and blahblahblahblahblah.''

She took a huge breath to replenish. "In other words, nothing new. Yours?"

He didn't answer right away, actually he couldn't. Or didn't want to. He stood there, grinning at her, letting delight wash over him. And even though delight was a total girly emotion, damned if she didn't delight him. He hadn't felt this buzzed since…the last time he'd seen her. Only clinching a big deal came close to a Laine high.

"Hello?" She quirked an eyebrow and leaned forward as if to inspect his skull for some sign of occupation. "Your mom and stepdad? How are they?"

He bent to match her movement, so their faces were only inches apart. She blinked in surprise, then her sexy mouth curved up and she lifted her other brow expectantly.

"Let's see." He dropped his gaze to her grin, then back up to her eyes. Blue and enticing, black-lashed and mischievous. He'd spent so much time inside them that staring at her up close this way felt like coming back to a place he'd always loved. "Paris this month, Costa Rica in the fall, concerts, parties, gardening, dinners at the club, sorry, can't talk long, the Harrises are due any minute, you remember Bob, don't you, head of his class at Harvard, he's now CEO of his own Fortune 500 company. In other words…"

"Nothing new." She laughed, then lingered long enough to dart a glance at his mouth and straightened. "Come on in and see the palace."

"Yes, ma'am." He followed with his bags, staring unapologetically at the sway of her firm rear, imagining himself into the beginnings of an erection. God, what pigs men were. He should be asking her how she was doing, where her life had been, where it was going, not salivating over her ass. But damn it, the woman had one fine ass.

They passed the tiny kitchen area to the left and entered the living room straight ahead, where Laine put the vase on a glass-topped coffee table, picked up what must be last week's fading bouquet and disappeared into the kitchen to dump it. Regardless of what Laine said, this Ben guy must have reason to think he'd caught the scent to heaven. No guy was that much of a sap otherwise.

Grayson parked his stuff against a beige couch and looked around. Hardwood floors with the Oriental rug she bought in Murray Hill a few years after college, TV in a wooden cabinet whose open doors revealed a disarray of workout tapes and chick movies and a white ceramic lamp that had belonged to her mother. Against one wall stood the dining table; above it hung the detailed print of the Sacre Coeur she'd bought on a high school trip to Paris. He glanced at the overstuffed armchair he and Laine had found on a curb, hauled up to her old apartment together and had re-upholstered. He ran his hand over the armrest. The chair probably wasn't worth a cent, but to them it had been the fantasy of stumbling over a discarded priceless antique.

Other unfamiliar things must be new acquisitions or belong to her roommate. He walked to the huge windows and pushed aside the sheer white curtains. Pretty decent cityscape thanks to the low buildings around them. Though he bet she used to be able to see the Twin Towers out this window.

He grimaced, then dropped the curtain and turned when he heard her come back into the room. She stood near the couch, clear eyes on him, shooting off her patented Laine energy even standing still. If he didn't know how amazing it was to be a whole lot closer, he'd swear he could be happy standing here watching her for the rest of the day. God he'd missed her. Didn't realize how much until he saw her again. No wonder he still dreamed about her. He was ready to dive back in without even knowing where they'd land.

"Want to see the rest of the place?"

"Sure." He picked up his bags and followed her down the hallway, not understanding the mischievous smile she shot back until she gestured him into a small, unbearably feminine bedroom with flowered curtains and matching yellow bedspread and rug.

"Wow." He put his bags down and surveyed the room, wondering if he'd emerge from this summer with the urge to wear panty hose. "This is so extra special."

"I knew you'd like it." Laine laughed behind him. "You're so fetching in pastels."

He sent her a grin over his shoulder. "It's fine. It's just what I need, Laine. And thanks for agreeing to let me use it."

"Well, it helps me out, too."

He turned, deciding he really liked being in a bedroom with her again. "You scratch mine, I'll scratch yours?"

"Something like that." She cocked her head and gave him a strange Mona Lisa smile. "Come see the rest? Or do you want to unpack?"

"Nothing to unpack really, since I'm only staying tonight this time." He pulled off his tie and threw it on the yellow bedspread, slipped slowly out of his jacket, watching for her reaction. "I am dying to get out of this suit, though."

"Okay." She took a step back and paused in the doorway. "I have a couple of e-mails to send, then we can have dinner."

He tossed his jacket on the bed and started to unbutton his shirt, giving her what they used to call the Green Light Grin. "What, you don't want to stay and watch me change?"

"Ha!" She rolled her eyes to the ceiling, then directed them down to his chest as if she couldn't help wanting to see it again. "You'll never change."

"Ah, Laine, but would you want me to?" He tossed the shirt over the jacket and slowly started to unbuckle his belt, watching her, waiting for when she'd start darting those hungry glances down.

Instead she paused and looked thoughtful, apparently taking the question more seriously than expected. He stopped in the middle of unzipping his fly. He did not want to hear this answer standing in his underwear.

"I guess not."

"Okay." He hadn't a clue how to respond. She *guessed* not? How was he supposed to take that? "I'll just be a sec."

She nodded and left, turning to the right, away from the living room toward what must be her bedroom.

Well, okay. He hadn't seen her for five years, maybe it was unreasonable to expect that the sight of him in an undershirt would send her into paroxysms of lust. But he knew Laine. She could jump-start into sexual arousal like nothing he'd ever seen. Sometimes all it took was the Green Light Grin to get her going.

He'd loved touching her, exploring her body, but unlike other women, it wasn't so much foreplay as teasing.

Grayson shrugged, took off his pants and undershirt, and hung the suit in the closet next to a brilliant array of female suits and cocktail dresses. Just because he could shake off the years apart at first sight didn't mean the same was true for her.

He pulled on jeans and a collarless teal polo shirt, a near duplicate of one Laine had bought him shortly before he'd moved away, saying she was sick of him wearing neutral colors. Finally, unpacked and feeling cooler, he scooped up his bathroom supplies and made his way in the direction Laine had gone, found the bathroom and grinned at the nearly bare counter and cabinet.

His ex-girlfriend in Chicago, Meg, had an entire drugstore in her bathroom. Cosmetics and lotions and cleaners—no, excuse him, *cleansers*—and polishes and waxes and miracle creams and toners, whatever the hell those were, plus puffs and poufs and wipes and assorted metal instruments of torture. No amount of persuasion convinced her she looked fine as is, maybe even better without all that crap slathered on. The fountain of youth was alive and well in the human brain, not in a million dollars' worth of merchandise. Someone like Laine would still be a young woman at age eighty-five.

He emerged from the bathroom and headed for the only doorway left unexplored in the place. Laine's bedroom. Where he hoped to be spending a lot of time this summer.

The room was evocatively familiar. She still had the queen mattress they'd bought together—in the same walnut frame—the same rose-colored bed-spread, right now strewn with pamphlets and magazines, still had her grandmother's dark wood dresser and the matching antique vanity. New to her setup, though—a computer workstation and a more up-to-date PC than the one she'd used when they were together.

At this PC, staring intently at the screen, sat Laine, sucking on a lollipop—ever the snack addict. Even though the door was open, he knocked.

"Come in." She swiveled her chair toward him and smiled. "Got everything you need?"

He bit back the obvious answer and gestured around the room. "This looks awfully familiar."

"Same old stuff. I'll just be a second here, then we can have a beer."

"Beer sounds fine." He moved toward the bed and picked up a handful of printed material. "What's all this?"

"I'm planning all kinds of fun this summer. Stuff I've always wanted to do but never had time."

"You're doing *all* this?" He shuffled through the magazines. "Yoga? Pottery? Cooking school? Dance classes? *Skydiving?*"

"Yup." She hit a key, closed out the window on her screen and jumped up, coming to stand next to him. "Cool, huh? That skydiving place looks amazing. They're booked up for a few weeks, but I think I'll sign up. You only need a half hour of instruction, then you can do a tandem jump with one of the instructors."

"Wow." He was already envious of the instructors. Her scent was getting to him; she was slightly nearsighted and stood close to see the magazines. If he moved his left arm, he'd probably brush against her breast.

"And this." She took the lollipop out of her mouth, reached to point, and her breast brushed against his tricep all by itself. "Is the yoga class I signed up for. Judy takes it, too. She says it's changed her life."

"Really." He was barely listening, just taking her in, the sweet smell of cherry lollipop, the warmth of her nearness, the softness of her breast on his arm.

"And this." Another point to another publication, another brush. "Is a place where you can sign up for cooking lessons. The woman running the place teaches French, Thai, a whole bunch of cuisines. Each session gives instructions for a complete meal. And this…"

Enough torture. He dumped the magazines back on the bed, lifted her under the arms and swung her against the wall.

"Grayson!" His name came out slightly garbled from the lollipop shoved against her cheek. "What are you doing?"

"I was wondering—" he grinned at her breathless tone, the darkening of her eyes, and looked down at her mouth, the white paper stick pressed firmly between her sexy lips "—when you were going to offer me a suck."

She snorted with surprised laughter, nearly losing the lollipop. He commandeered it and pushed it slowly into his own mouth. "Mmm, cherry. My favorite."

"You are awful. Give me that."

"Okay." He took it out of his mouth, held it out

of reach when she tried to grab it back. "Open your mouth."

"Grayson…"

"Open."

She stared at him for a second with an expression he couldn't read, then opened her mouth. He licked the candy one more time, then painted it, sticky and wet, across her lips.

She sucked her breath in sharply and froze. Grayson suppressed a smile of triumph. He had her right where he wanted her. Remembering a certain other lollipop—grape, as he recalled—that he'd drawn over her lips just like this, then back into his mouth to moisten like a water-colorist dipping his brush into water. Then he'd painted the candy again over her nipples, around her navel, between her legs, leisurely sucking off the sticky sweetness after each application.

This time she licked her own lips clean and grabbed for the sucker, which he held out of her reach again.

"Say please," he said in the low whisper he used when they were playing sex games, when he'd make her beg.

"No. Grayson…" She pressed back against the wall, eyes wide, face flushed, but not with pleasure. She looked confused, troubled.

Immediately he let her go, put the lollipop back in her mouth and held up his hands in surrender. "Sorry. Just playing."

"I know. It's just…" She laughed uneasily, grabbed the stick and crunched the lollipop into bits. "Well, how about that beer now?"

"Beer sounds fine." He followed her to the tiny

kitchen, uneasy, deflated, and perched on a stool across the tile counter. What was that about? She still wanted him, she'd responded, but something was keeping her back. "Are you seeing someone?"

She put two bottles on the counter and turned to fish through a drawer. He picked one, gave the top a mighty twist and let go in a hurry, shaking his hand to ease the sting.

"Opener?" She pushed one across the counter and leaned forward on folded arms. "No, I'm not seeing anyone…yet."

Yet? "Ben."

"No, not Ben. I told you not Ben."

He shrugged with a nonchalance he didn't feel, pulled open the top to her beer, then his and took a long swallow, watching the top of her bent head. "Then who?"

"I don't know yet."

He paused with the bottle against his lip. "You don't know."

"Well some friends and I…some online friends from this reading group, Eve's Apple…" She gestured aimlessly, then clutched the beer bottle in both hands. "We split off from the main group and we're…looking for Men To Do."

"Men to *do?*"

"Men To Do Before Saying I Do."

He lowered the bottle to the counter, his taste for beer gone. "Work with me here, Laine. What the hell are you talking about?"

"We want to find men who are totally inappropriate for marriage—or even relationships—and…" She waggled her eyebrows.

"Do them."

"Yup." She straightened suddenly and opened a cabinet behind her. "You hungry?"

"No." He folded his arms across his chest. Call him a caveman, call him irrationally possessive, call him whatever you wanted, he did not like the sound of this. "So you haven't found a man yet?"

"Not yet." She brought down a bag of sourdough pretzels, her mood entirely too cheerful for his taste. "I've found some possibles, though."

"Where? Wait, don't tell me. Men To Do magazine? MenToDo.com? The Men To Do Show?"

She tore open the bag and rolled her eyes, then walked around the counter and sat on the stool next to him. "NYdates.com."

"Okay." He pictured her e-mailing furiously in her bedroom just now and felt vaguely sick. "So what happens next?"

She crunched on a pretzel. "I find someone I like, we write back and forth, and if he sounds good, then I go meet him for a drink or dinner or something."

"And do him."

She chased the pretzel with a swallow of beer. "Yeah, if it works out."

"And will you tell this guy that you're just 'doing' him and not interested in anything more than that?"

"Like a guy would care?"

He narrowed his eyes. "Okay, you got me on that one."

She laughed and punched him playfully; he caught her hand and pulled her off the stool, opened his legs and brought her in just between his knees. "You sure this is a good idea?"

"It's perfect. Just right for my summer of fun." She tried to pull away, but he kept her there, hands at her slim waist, dying to pull her forward flush against him but not wanting to upset her again.

"What if you meet a psycho?"

"Honey, I already dated you, what's a psycho going to do?"

"Ha." He tightened his hold, pulled her toward him another inch, and splayed his fingers along the sides of her body. "I don't want you to get hurt."

She gave a forced laugh. "Too bad you didn't feel that way when we were together."

He started, shocked at the bitterness in her tone even though her expression stayed teasing. Okay. Maybe the past hadn't been laid to rest on a lot of levels, but he wasn't digging all that crap up now. "We're talking about you and the Neanderthals of New York."

"Getting hurt is not an option. These will be deliberately inappropriate men. The only thing involved will be my body."

He suppressed a primal growl and moved his thumbs up and down her firm stomach, noting her sudden stillness with satisfaction. "So when you bring these guys home to do, can I watch?"

"Ha." She gave a distracted grin as if she was responding on autopilot. "I don't *think* so."

He moved his thumbs up her rib cage, tugged her in even closer. "Maybe press a glass to the wall and listen?"

"Pervert." She mumbled the word somewhat dreamily.

"Because I wouldn't really need to see, if I could hear." He spoke softly, moved his hands slowly up until his thumbs would be able to brush across her breasts if he extended them. "I already know the noises you make. I'd know when you were getting close, when you make that whimpering sound like nothing else in the world matters to you right then but coming.''

''Stop.'' She was whispering, too, still motionless, caught.

''Stop what?'' He was getting hard touching her, talking about her, picturing how she looked right before she came. ''What am I doing?''

She pushed away and went back around to her side of the counter, grabbed her beer and shoved her hand into the bag of pretzels. ''Trying to get into my pants.''

''So what's your point?'' He meant the comment playfully, but his dick was hard, he wanted her, it looked as if that wasn't going to happen right now, he didn't understand why not, and it pissed him off.

''My point is that my pants are off limits.''

''From what I just heard, it sounds like freaking open season.''

''Not for you, Grayson. Been there, done you, not going there again.''

She said the words calmly, looking right into his eyes. He tightened his mouth, felt a reflexive jerk in his gut. That time she was serious. Her body might still want him, but her brain was firmly opposed.

''Okay. Message received and understood.''

''Good.'' She let out a breath and grinned a sweet grin he was in no mood to return. ''Now that's out of the way, are you hungry?''

She turned and reached up into another cabinet; the gesture parted her shirt and skirt, exposing smooth skin and accentuating the curve of her gorgeous ass.

"Yeah, I'm hungry."

She had no idea how hungry. But damn it, getting the meal he wanted was going to be much more of a challenge than he thought.

4

From: Angie Keller
Sent: Tuesday
To: Laine Blackwell; Kathy Baker
Subject: Re: Men To Do and (ack!) Old Boy-
friend Returns

Hey, girl. I'd say you have yourself a winner with this Antonio guy. Mmm-mmm, them's good eatin'. If things don't work out, you can send him on down here to North Carolina, and I'll show the boy how to boogie.

But what I really want is to see pictures of this ex of yours, butt-naked if possible. And come on, give Angie a break. You're planning to live with this guy all summer who was heaven-on-earth to screw and nothing's gonna happen? Yeow! I'm betting the air was pretty darn thick when he walked in. Or maybe you two have already revisited paradise? That kind of chemistry doesn't just get up and walk away.

Heck, girl, live a little! Two at once. Vain Foreigner and the Gray Stud.

Just make sure to send details. And pictures. And detailed pictures.

Me, I'm still prowling the bars of Asheville,

N.C. No luck last night unless you count the drooling icky married guy, but come the weekend, I'm there again.

God bless,
Angie

From: Kathy Baker
Sent: Tuesday
To: Laine Blackwell; Angie Keller
Subject: The Vain Foreigner and Old Boyfriend

Of course I'm not such a god-awful slut-puppy as Angie, so I'll say hey, the Vain Foreigner person sounds good and looks yummy, but Auntie Kathy just has to chime in and say be careful. Don't give him your phone number or address or even your last name. And don't let him pick you up at your apartment—meet him at the restaurant or wherever you go. And if you've done all that, then I've done my Auntie Duty, so have fun! And tell all when you come home. *If* you come home (nyuck nyuck).

As for this boyfriend-type person, hmm. Danger there, I won't say more, but I'll be curious to see how it all pans out. And yeah, how about treating us to a picture of him, too?

Me, I have a guy at work that would make a perfect Man To Do, but I think taking co-workers to bed is right up there in the stupidity department with handing steak through the bars of a lion's cage (typed "bras of a lion's cage" the first time. Hello?). So I will continue to search far and afield (is that the right expression? What field? Where?) for my man.

Hmm…maybe the hunky UPS guy who just pulled up…

Gotta go!

Kathy

LAINE LIFTED the ten-pound weight up, then down, up, then down, working her biceps, following the chirpy instructions of the exercise instructor on the video. Laine needed a workout in a big way this morning; she'd slept like crap knowing Grayson was in the next bedroom, and woke with a tired and bleary brain. Thank goodness he'd left early, gone already when she got up at eight. She was not in the mood to handle the all-too-familiar intimacy of a shared morning.

Up for two, down for two, hold for a pulse of three. She finished working her arm, got the matching weight and moved both to her shoulders for leg work. Then the other arm. Aerobic intervals. More leg work—squats, lunges, dips. Her body felt good, clean and strong, the weights satisfyingly tough to handle. And her brain was responding slowly, returning from its Grayson-induced disorientation.

Seeing him had been totally different than she'd expected. Instead of the sisterly affection she was so sure would comprise her now and future feelings, the second she opened the door and saw him standing there—masculine, magnetic, full of life—she'd been shot back into her own past, which she'd worked so hard to leave behind. Yeesh. The rest of the evening, even when he wasn't coming on to her—force of habit for God's sake, the man was a walking pass— she'd been struggling against the pull of what they'd been together.

She draped herself on all fours over her exercise step, fitted a three-pound weight behind her knee and bent her leg to keep it in place. Lift and down, lift and down, sixteen reps, then up and cross over the other leg for eight. Her deepest fear? If the initial thrill of seeing him didn't fade, she might find out, to her ultimate horror, that she hadn't managed to put him on the shelf after all. That couldn't happen. If she didn't get herself under control, she'd be toast. Burned black. Never survive the summer.

Leg reps over, she sat back to stretch, then lay on one side and started working her adductor muscles, the three-pound weight now resting on her outer thigh. Lift leg, lower, lift, lower, toe pointed down. She couldn't think that way, couldn't even acknowledge the possibility that her feelings weren't dead and buried. She was older and wiser now, understood exactly why she and Grayson had been bad together.

For him, it was always about the chase. When they'd been legitimate boyfriend and girlfriend in college, he'd been so passionate, so into her, so sincere. She'd gradually come to trust him and fallen hard, finally told him she loved him, that she could see their future working out together. Complete capitulation, end of chase. He'd given a hunted smile and run off to immerse himself in a French kissathon with Joanne Randle, which Laine had been lucky enough to walk in on a few hours later. Such fun.

After that she'd slammed her emotional door shut, locked her heart safely away from him and away from the pain that little incident had produced—more than she would have thought possible. They'd never even sat down to discuss what had happened, apart from the first few accusatory shouting matches. And even though she'd been crazy enough, or helpless enough, or hooked enough to allow their sexual relationship to continue on and off for years before he moved away, she'd never allowed those deep-down feelings to resurface entirely. On the few occasions when she'd slipped, became too tender, made assumptions about the future, even in terms of weeks, he'd bolt and she wouldn't hear from him. For a week or two, a month, two months, three... Then he'd call, and she'd go back like an addict unable to quit.

She finished stretching the other leg, lay on her back and began the killer abdominal crunch series. However— Hello. Attention, please—in the past five years she'd made tremendous strides, and she was no longer so crazy or hooked or helpless as to let him pull her back into that kind of destructive pattern again. If for no other reason than because Grayson was still so much the same.

Within a minute of his arrival he'd jumped to the conclusion that the only thing on Ben's mind was sex, which would of course be correct if Grayson were the flower-sender. Nothing she said would change his mind. Then he tried to manipulate her into resuming a sexual relationship—didn't ask, didn't invite, manipulated. Assumed she would still respond to him the same way—okay, never mind that she did—that she'd jump right back in, no questions asked, nothing to discuss. And he was still the champion of suppressing his emotions to cool, in-control masculinity—like pretending her Men To Do scheme didn't bother him.

Oh, please.

She'd had the distinct satisfaction of watching his okay-you-can-worship-my-bod-all-over-again routine crack and nearly fall apart.

The video instructor mercifully stopped and Laine flopped back, letting her body relax into the glow of fatigue. Stretches done, she headed for her bedroom, stripped, tossed her workout clothes onto her bed and jumped into the shower, exulting in the lukewarm stream on her heated body.

Honesty time? Yeah, she'd been worshiping his bod. Surreptitiously she hoped. What a bod it was. Only better now that he'd bulked into real manhood. When he'd started undressing in Monica's room, she'd been hard-put to leave. Which meant she'd sort of responded the way he assumed she would. That damn lollipop trick—he knew just what buttons to push. Knew when he dragged the wet candy across her lips, she'd instantly start reliving the first time. The way he'd licked the lollipop—that one was grape—painted it on various parts of her body, then sucked the flavor off her skin. The way he'd dipped it all the way inside her, then put it back in his mouth, circled her clit and sucked off the melted sweetness...she'd come within seconds. Practically set the bed on fire.

Laine blew out a breath and reminded herself to move. She turned the knob to stop the shower, opened the curtain, then stared at the water running out of the tub faucet.

Oh, it was just *too* tempting.

She grinned, sank down and scooted close, leaning back on her elbows. Dropping her head back, she let the warm splashing stream play between her spread legs. Within seconds her breathing grew rough, her hips arched. The stimulation was warm, liquid and so intense. She gasped, felt the climax building, gasped again and moaned. Nearly there. Nearly there. Nearly…

The door burst open. She squealed and rolled to the side, huddled down in the tub and peeked over the edge, heart racing. Grayson. In suspiciously tented running shorts and nothing else.

"What the hell are you doing?"

"Sorry." He backed toward the door. "I was, uh…"

"Spying, you creep." Laine lunged to the end of the tub, grabbed her towel and stood, wrapping it around her, brain enraged, body bewildered by being jerked away from its anticipated completion. "Damn it, Grayson, we are going to make rules around here."

"I'm sorry. I really am." He held his hands up in surrender, dark eyes earnest, face and hair damp with perspiration from his run. "I wasn't sure you were here, I pressed against the door to listen and it gave on me."

"Oh, right." Her gaze skittered over his chest and back to his eyes. Grrrrr. Why did she have to check *that* out? "It didn't occur to you to knock?"

"Next time I will." His eyes flicked to the water still pouring out of the tap and took on a wicked gleam. "Still your favorite method?"

She bent, blushing furiously, one hand pressing her towel in place, and yanked off the faucets. The guy knew way too much about her. "I was just turning off the shower when you barged in on me."

"Really." He crossed his arms over his fantastic chest, which made the stupid part of her brain still wanting that orgasm send her eyes down again. "Turning off the shower makes you moan like that?"

She narrowed her eyes. "You *were* listening, you pig."

"I heard. I wasn't listening. There's a diff—"

"Hair-splitting pig."

"That's *Mr.* Hair-Splitting Pig to you."

She fought off laughter, clutched the towel in both fists, face still hot, body trembling. This was exactly Grayson's operating mode: sneaking around, coming from behind—figuratively, she meant—to try to get what he was after. Well she wasn't playing that game anymore. "Okay, you're done, you've apologized, you can go."

His eyes dropped from hers to her bare shoulders, wandered across her well-covered breasts, sauntered down suggestively further, then back up to her eyes, with that look of sleepy desire he was so freaking good at that her freaking traitorous body responded, *Oh, goody, here's what we want, let's get started.*

She swallowed loud enough to be heard and pointed to the exit. "Go."

"Okay." He nodded, his voice low and husky, turned, then paused in the doorway, head to one side. "You still make me crazy."

She stared at the door closing behind him, at the crack in the ivory paint that looked like a clumsily drawn bolt of lightning. She wanted to throw something after him, to hear it crash against the wall and thud to the ground, to yell, to throw him out for good. He'd engineered the entire episode, from pushing open the door once he figured out what she was up to, to saying she made him crazy just before his convenient exit. He'd intended to leave her stunned and drooling after him. Pig, pig and double, triple pig.

He made her a *lot* crazier than she made him. And

not crazy in the same way he meant. But he wouldn't take control of her again. Absolutely not, either sexually or emotionally. She had let him go and he was going to stay gone.

Taking a deep breath and holding the towel firmly around her, she sailed out of the bathroom and into her room, closed the door behind her and made sure it latched properly in case Peeping Tom decided he wanted more sicko action.

She dropped the towel and rummaged in her bureau for shorts and a shirt. All she had structured today was a badly needed yoga class this evening. The rest of the day she'd stay maniacally busy to recenter herself. She'd go to the bookstore to buy what she needed for her French class, get tap shoes, visit a museum or the library.

But before any of that, right now, she had one all-important task that couldn't be put off a second longer.

Making a hot do-me date with Antonio Salvo.

LAINE HURRIED UP the sidewalk to 110 Waverly Place, Babbo Restaurant. She was ten minutes late—she hated being late—but it was beyond her to decide what to wear. Nothing too seductive in case the chemistry with Antonio was horrible and she only wanted to end the evening with a handshake. But she didn't want to look too anti-femme-fatale, either, in case she wanted the party to go on all night. In the end, she'd decided on a simple turquoise shift and low-heeled tan sandals.

She paused, her hand on the door and took a deep breath, pretending composure she didn't feel. *Okay. Here we go.*

One step inside, a quick glance around the entrance and she saw him; he stood at her approach. Her first impression—he wasn't tall enough. A good four inches shorter than Grayson. Her second—he was oh-yum powerfully built. Third, when she met his eyes—*wow*. Blue-gray, nearly silver, and some hot-damn chemistry to go with them.

Oh, *yes*.

She held out her hand, which he took, gazing deeply into her eyes and making her go liquid and shaky. His dark hair looked different from the photograph posted on NYdates.com. Wavier and parted in the middle, which she could not think of a single reason any male would want to do. And he had a goatee thing going on. Not her favorite. A vision of Grayson's clean, male-smelling jawline had to be pushed firmly out of her mind. This evening was *not* about Grayson.

"Hi, Antonio, sorry I'm late."

"It's okay. Very nice to meet you." His voice was less than deep, stopping just short of nasal. He smiled a dynamite smile, his sexy gaze lingering on hers so she had to look away. *Mmm*. The hair issues were definitely dwindling in importance. Thank. Goodness. *Grayson, eat your heart out.*

Ten minutes later they had settled at a romantic table for two—a tiny bit too close to the romantic tables for two on either side, but, oh well, that was New York—and had ordered drinks. Well, *he'd* ordered for both of them before she could open her mouth, but who could object to champagne? He'd also taken off his gray silk jacket, hung it carefully over the back of his chair, and his biceps positively bulged out the sleeves of the black turtleneck he wore tucked into black linen pants. *Most* impressive. She could sit here imagining him naked and the meal would fly by quite happily.

"Cheers." He lifted his champagne flute and toasted her. "Here's to getting to know each other."

"Absolutely." She clinked the glass and returned his game-show-host smile, all atingle. Getting to know each other in the carnal sense, especially. Despite the hair flaws and the fact that he did not have the slightest hint of an Italian accent—so she hadn't a clue why he'd been so insistent that he was from Italy—he was perfect.

She scanned the long and complicated menu and her eyes started to glaze over. Grayson loved fancy restaurants, while she was more a diner kind of girl. Not that she didn't enjoy complicated flavors, she just wasn't one to wake up craving beef cheek ravioli.

"I'll order for you, okay? I eat here all the time, I know what you'll like."

"Oh...well..." She hid a grimace and closed her menu. First the drinks, now the entire meal...if she had to use the rest room would he offer to do that for her, too? And how would he know what she liked after ten minutes of talking about nothing? "That would be fine, Antonio, thank you."

She didn't have to live with the guy, just get him into bed.

"Terrific. You won't be sorry, I promise you."

The waiter showed up and Antonio ordered what sounded like enough food to last a lifetime. The waiter listened carefully, inclined his head and hurried away.

Laine took another sip of the delicious champagne, then plonked her elbows on the table, stared fetch-

ingly over her clasped hands into Antonio's stud-of-
life eyes and uttered the second most powerful sentence in every woman's arsenal.

"So, Antonio, tell me about yourself."

Half an hour later, after marinated fresh anchovies
with beet chips in lobster oil, he was just getting to
his senior year in high school. Sports trophies. The
beginning of his life as a weight lifter. His dynamite
grades. The women who had hurt him. Laine sipped
champagne, ate the delicious fresh fish and nodded,
tsk-tsked and awwwed at appropriate moments. She
could feel the flush of alcohol on her cheeks, the tiny
breath of air on her bare shoulders when someone
passed behind her and the sexual awareness of Antonio's stunning masculinity slowly beginning to sink
under the weight of his verbiage.

But.

He was exactly what she wanted for her Man To
Do, right? A man she had little in common with but
chemistry, and she and Antonio had that in spades. A
man she could no more fall in love with than whip
up beef cheek ravioli herself. He was perfect. All she
had to do was weather the conversational part of the
evening and get him into bed. Easy breezy.

Except that halfway through his college career, in
pure self-defense, she allowed her thoughts to
wander, though she carefully kept her oh-you-are-*so*-
fascinating face pasted on. Was Grayson back in her
condo after his day of meetings? Thinking about her
out on her date? She hoped Antonio wouldn't mind
if they went back to his place. No way would she let
herself in for Grayson's reaction to him.

Champagne over, on to a gutsy white wine. Goat
cheese tortellini with dried orange and fennel pollen.

Antonio appeared to be winding down college, but then, what do you know, he did a year of graduate school in Engineering. Laine slipped off her shoes under the table and rubbed her feet happily on the smooth carpet. Was there anything she was forgetting that she'd need tonight? She'd worn sexy underwear, had a purse full of condoms…which reminded her, she needed more shampoo when she went to the drugstore next week. And her period was coming up, so she better check her tampon supply when she got home tomorrow…

Graduate school and goat cheese over, a monologue on Antonio's impressive and many-branched family tree began. Red wine followed white. Lamb chops followed pasta. And still, the Saga of Antonio would not die.

She did manage to interject a sentence or two once in a while, enough to make him feel they were having a real conversation. No, she'd never been to Italy. Yes, she'd like to go, but England was first on her travel list. Yes, she'd seen *Die Hard* but, hmm, no, she couldn't agree it was the best movie ever made. Well, the cruise he went on sounded lovely, but she was a vacation-in-the-mountains kind of person. Yes, she was sure his mother made delicious calamari, but she couldn't get past the tentacles.

And on…and on…

Until finally chestnut spice cake with pears and caramel mascarpone. And coffee. And brandy. And Laine insisting to the point of rudeness on splitting the check, and finally giving in and letting him pay. *Fine. Be that way.*

There was only one way now to salvage the already-endless evening.

She walked with him out onto Waverly Place, into the cool first-day-of-summer breeze, her spirits revived, and sent him a shy and provocative look. "That was delicious, Antonio, thank you."

"You're welcome." He grinned down at her shy and provocative look and took her hand. His was large and strong and slightly moist. "We should do it again sometime. Soon."

"I'd like that." She moved closer and made sure he could feel her breast against his enormous arm.

Immediately she thought of the same contact between her breast and Grayson's somewhat less enormous arm. It hadn't been on purpose that time, at least not at first, but God, it had been exciting. About as exciting as this...wasn't.

Stop that. Not fair to judge Antonio on one breast brush. She and Grayson had the unfair advantage of a lot of incredible chemical memories. Besides, her date tonight was a different scenario entirely, with no emotions involved. Just because she couldn't quite manage to be panting with desire right off the bat, the way she always was with—

Never mind.

She was going to go through with this regardless. For one thing, she couldn't go home and face Grayson without scoring tonight. Not, as she had already pointed out, that this had anything to do with him. But this was her summer of fun, this was her Man To Do. He was terrifically handsome, built to last all night, and even if he was a tad overbearing and not the most fascinating person—wait, especially *because* he was a tad overbearing and not the most fascinating person—she was going to do him even if it killed her.

"So, Antonio."

"Yes, Laine." He sent her that supercharged grin and made her wonder vaguely about a teeth-whitening kit she'd seen on an infomercial.

"I was wondering…" She smiled her best sexual smile back to him. "If you'd like to…go somewhere now."

His brows dropped down in apparent confusion. "Like where?"

"Mmm, maybe your place?"

Scowling, he came to a standstill in the street, backed her toward the curb to avoid being bumped by strolling pedestrians and put his hands on his hips. "My place."

"Yes." She took a sultry step toward him, traced his massive forearm through his jacket, up his arm, over the hills and valleys of biceps and triceps and delts to his rock-solid shoulder. Oh, my goodness, this man could probably accomplish pretty much any position anyone had ever thought of. "I was thinking we could get to know each other…even better."

She tilted her head invitingly, pouted her lips superbly sensually to rival Renee Zellweger's best effort, and waited.

"What do you mean?" His scowl became more definite.

She gave a silent growl of frustration. For God's sake, how dense could he be? "I think you know what I mean, Antonio."

"No." He folded his arms across his chest. "I don't. Explain."

Laine's superbly sensual expression froze. It was *not* supposed to be this hard to seduce a man. She'd never had the slightest trouble before. In fact, come to think of it, she'd never even had to *do* it before. It shouldn't even be *necessary*.

"Okay. How's this." She took a deep breath, trying to keep the exasperation out of her voice. "I was thinking that you and I could go back to your place right now and have sex until we can no longer walk upright."

His face closed into rage. For a terrifying second she thought he was actually going to become violent.

He took two steps away from her, as if he just found out she had the plague, and raised his arm to point. "You slut."

Passersby began to look interested. Laine dropped her head onto her hand. Oh, this was just freaking dandy. With all the easy lays in NYC, she had to land a damn choir boy.

"Antonio, I didn't—"

"I thought you were a nice girl."

"I *am* a nice girl. There's nothing *not nice* about wanting—" She glanced around at the way-too-interested bystanders. "You know. That."

"Where I come from, there is."

"Antonio, you come from Brooklyn."

He put a fist to his extremely impressive chest, which she now would not get a chance to see let alone touch and/or taste. Though somehow that wasn't overwhelming her with sadness. "In my heart I am from a small Italian village in the mountains of Sicily. Girls like you are—"

"Look." Laine lifted her hands, fingers spread as if they itched to latch on to a certain thick, veiny neck and squeeze not at all gently. "Just plain no would be fine. I understand no. I respect no. Unlike most of your gender, I even know what it means."

Antonio spat on the sidewalk in front of her, turned on his heel and strode away to the amused murmur of the crowd.

Laine rolled her eyes. *Oh, for crying out—*

"Hey, babe." A stocky guy with a big leer and aftershave strong enough to clear Yankee Stadium stepped up to her. "I'd be glad to help you out."

Laine shot him her fiercest I-don't-brake-for-creeps stare, and he backed off, shoulders raised in a long shrug. "Can't blame a guy for trying."

Yes, in fact, tonight she could. Tonight she could blame pretty much anyone for anything. Starting with herself for thinking this was a good idea.

She turned in the opposite direction from the way Mr. Huffy Sicily had gone and walked quickly to leave the sniggering New Yorkers behind, before she pulled out her cell phone, dialed Judy's number and stepped into the street to hail a cab.

Miraculously a taxi pulled up before Judy even answered. Laine hurled herself inside and barked her address to the driver who pulled off.

"'Lo?"

"Judy, it's Laine. Date. From. Hell. The guy was a totally chauvinistic idiot."

"…oh, yeah?"

Laine could barely hear her. She buckled her seat belt, tightening the strap to a nearly painful degree. "He ordered *for* me, drinks *and* dinner, talked about *nothing* but himself the entire night, insisted on paying, and *then*…" She paused for effect.

"What?"

Laine swept her arm across the back seat. "He wouldn't even *sleep* with me."

The cabdriver jerked a glance up into his rear-view mirror. Laine turned to watch Eighth Avenue speed by.

"He wouldn't?"

"No. Can you believe that? He was supposed to be my Man To Do, and he wouldn't even do me."

"Well, that's—"

"Plus." She switched the phone to her other ear. "Plus, Grayson's over tonight, and now I have to go back early and listen to him gloat."

"Wow, Laine, I—"

"Not that this is about Grayson, of course it's not. It's about Muscles Mussolini and his Medieval Morality."

"Uh-huh."

Laine narrowed her eyes. "Why do you sound so skeptical?"

"Because I am. I'm also exhausted, I was up before dawn with cramps and you woke me."

Laine's eyes shot wide, and she smacked herself on the forehead. "Oh, jeez, Judy, I am so sorry. I just rattled on without even asking if it was a good time to call you. I'm really sorry."

"Don't worry. I'm sorry about the guy. But maybe he didn't like being treated like a piece of meat."

"A piece of—" Laine sent a frown out into the street, turned to the other window and sent another. Okay. Maybe she had been treating him like a…beef cheek. And maybe he hated that. But it was just her luck to find the only normal male in the city who would.

"And if it's not about Grayson, then why did his name jump into the conversation about fifteen seconds after it started?"

"Oh. Well, *that*. I mean…" She held her hand up

in the air, willing some brilliant ending to her sentence to come sailing out.

"Good night, Laine." Judy chuckled.

Laine dropped her hand to her side. Breath she hadn't realized she was holding left her in an emptying whoosh. "Good night. Sorry I woke you."

"Not a problem. Lunch Saturday?"

"Yes, of course. Sleep well." She flipped the phone off and stowed it back in her purse, then rearranged her skirt and shifted on the seat.

Okay. She needed to deal with facts.

Fact one: she had not scored a Man To Do tonight.

Fact two: she was going to have to go home to her apartment and deal with the Smug One.

Fact three... She leaned her head back on the seat and stared at the taxi ceiling. As sexy as Antonio had been, she'd admit—only to herself—that she was relieved when he turned her down. Not that sex with him would have been awful, it would have been fine. But even with the terrific chemistry they had going, imagining that kind of intimacy with him hadn't ever felt...right.

She sighed and rolled down the window to let the city's night air into the stale car interior. Even when she'd had other boyfriends over the years, other lovers, it hadn't ever felt really right. Not the way it had with—

No. Not him again.

The cab passed a road crew putting down smelly asphalt. Laine rolled the window back up with a jerk. If Grayson was "right" then she wanted to be wrong for the rest of her life. Anything but a return to those endless rounds of hope and joy and pain and rejection.

So here was the plan. Go bravely up to her apartment, attempt to dodge questions, do a nice round of yoga to de-stress and refresh, and then move right along to NYdates.com.

To find a brand-new Man To Do.

5

GRAYSON TOOK A SIP of his martini and smiled in satisfaction. Tanqueray gin, very dry, with a twist. Nothing like that first icy-clean taste. He glanced at the pink, blue and green concoctions being served up at the end of the bar in glasses identical to his, and rolled his eyes. Martinis should not have girly colors or sweet crap in them. Next the trendy crowd would want their 'tinis frozen in a blender, with those little umbrellas for decoration.

He took another sip and leaned his arm on the dark wood of the upstairs bar at Proof on Third Avenue. He needed this drink. He always enjoyed a good martini, but he seldom felt anything like need. This evening was an exception. Today he'd had a meeting at Omega Source Industries. Big company with bigger potential, serving the medical and scientific community. He'd been cultivating them for weeks and had finally brought them to the point where they could see the value of starting to sell their products online. If he could land an account like that, a company with ongoing needs—training videos, marketing pieces, new product unveilings—his company would have a good foothold on the security it needed.

The meeting went well in every way. He and Chuck had made an excellent presentation, showed the Marketing V.P. from Omega several options. But ninety-nine percent of the time, Grayson could tell coming out of a meeting whether he'd get the sale or not, and his gut was telling him not this time. There'd been nothing more than maybe a slight lack of enthusiasm, a slight air of detachment from the V.P. who'd met with them.

Jameson Productions wasn't going to get this sale. Business went that way sometimes. Grayson would make the initial contact, he'd do all the work to get the potential client to broaden its thinking, he'd do up the marketing plan, sell them on the concepts— then they'd ask for bids on the project and some other multimedia company would waltz away with the prize Grayson's blood and sweat made possible. All was fair in love and war and sales.

Another sip. More of a gulp, really. He set the glass down, stared at the legs of alcohol running back into the glass, and the thought that had been trying to penetrate his consciousness all day long finally managed to burst through. Laine was out with Antonio the Italian Sex God. Right now. He shook his head and smiled without humor. He hoped she was having a really good time with her "Man To Do." Getting all the nice impersonal sex she seemed to need from anyone other than him.

A blonde came into view in his peripheral vision, sat at the bar two chairs away and looked over at him. He turned deliberately, met her gaze and returned her inviting smile. Well, well. Maybe Laine wasn't going to be the only one having fun tonight.

"Hello." Her voice was low and alluring, her features beautifully formed, hair streaked blond and fashionably tousled—she was definitely dressed for action, clothing and attitude.

"Hi." He glanced at her cleavage, which strained to escape a bright yellow tube top under a white sheer blouse. Yeah, he could get lost in there for a few hours. "I'm Grayson."

She held out her hand, turned down as if he was supposed to kiss instead of shake it. He shook. Her hand was limp, chilly, delicate and blue-veined, with red nails that could lacerate his back into ribbons.

"I'm Lorena, but you can call me Candy."

He nearly chuckled. *Of course I can.* "So, Candy, are you waiting for someone?"

"Maybe." Her eyes took a leisurely pleasure trip around his body. "Maybe you."

Oh yeah. He nodded, as if considering her words, taken aback slightly when his body didn't send the usual surge of testosterone excitement to accompany his brain's victory dance.

The burly bartender approached. Grayson acknowledged him and gestured to the woman beside him. "What are you drinking, Candy?"

"Ketel One Martini, *extra* dirty." She said the last words slowly, like a sexual offering, complete with pouting lips and a wink. The bartender's eyes widened; he glanced at Grayson and went off to make her drink.

Ah, a woman who drank real drinks. He liked that. He liked that very much.

"So…" Lorena/Candy oozed off her stool and oozed onto the one right next to him like a sensual snake-woman, brushing his knees with her thighs, half bared by a tiny red skirt.

In any other mood the frankly sexual approach and teasing contact would have made his dick wake up and prepare to get happy. But the old boy barely seemed to notice. And Grayson knew its hydraulic response to female stimulation was in full working order. Minutes after seeing Laine he'd been assured of that. The meeting today must have gotten to him more than he'd thought.

"So?"

She undulated her body closer, leaning to give him a private showing of her twin bounties, and reached to tap a red-tipped finger on his thigh. "Tell me about Grayson."

An uneasy feeling took root in his stomach. She was beautiful, willing, sexy as hell, and he wasn't responding. This hadn't happened to him in years. Not since he'd lived in New York the last time and had been involved on-again, off-again with—

He picked up his drink and attacked it with a vengeance.

Fifteen minutes later, fifteen minutes of drooping banter, flaccid get-to-know-you chatter and limp flirtation, he and his penis admitted defeat.

The last sip of his martini went down unpleasantly tepid and tasting like acid. He stood and replaced the glass on the bar. "Candy, it's been a pleasure."

"What?" She turned, her second martini still raised to her mouth, gazing at him over the rim in frank disbelief. "You're leaving?"

"I'm afraid so."

"Alone?"

"Yes."

Her eyes narrowed. "You're married."

"No, just—" *bored* "—tired. But thanks for the company."

"Right." She brushed off the surprise, already focusing on a suited single male a few chairs to her left. ''Sure thing.''

He picked up his laptop and briefcase and headed downstairs for the exit, around tables and between alcohol-infused bodies, then thankfully out into the fresh air and deepening twilight.

This sucked. Massively. Since when did he even hesitate when the game was on? Since— He didn't even want to think about it. Candy was not only incredibly attractive, but so willing it wouldn't even have been considered a hunt. But the whole episode had felt pre-programmed, utterly lacking in spontaneity. *I'm Grayson. Are you waiting for someone? What are you drinking?* Buy her the drink, chat, get slightly soused, go home together, have awkward unfamiliar sex and say goodbye. Same as the last one. Probably same as the next.

He wasn't in the mood for Candy. He wanted something unexpectedly fresh, fiery, salty, and still somehow infinitely sweet.

A cab responded to his raised arm; he got in and rode sulkily to Laine's apartment, greeted Roger the doorman, who—yeah, it just figured—had another damn bouquet for him to take up. All the way to the eighth floor in the slow, clanky elevator, pissed and crabby, he had to engage this fresh, joyously scented thing of beauty meant for Laine—and refrain from smashing it against the wall.

He let himself into her apartment and paused, listening, half hopeful the date had been a dud and she was home early, half afraid the date had been a smash and she was home early, writhing in the sheets with Italian salami. That would really cap his day. He'd go right back out and find Candy again, or a Candy clone, and who cared if he wasn't interested.

Another few silent seconds and he breathed again—though not in relief—carried the damn flowers into the living room and set them on the coffee table. Went to his room, changed into sweats and a T-shirt. Stalked to the kitchen. Got himself a beer, a box of crackers, a brick of cheese, flipped on the TV. Oh, this was going to be one hot evening.

He flipped through the channels, in the mood for bombs, explosions, blood—something with Schwarzenegger or Stallone, Vin Diesel or Van Damme.

There. *Terminator 2*. A crushed skull. Exploding bombs. Shooting lasers. Man's arm broken, man tossed onto kitchen grill. *Ahhhh*. Grayson leaned back on the couch, clutching the open box of wheat crackers, plonked his feet on the coffee table and sighed in satisfaction. Perfect.

Except he'd left his beer there on the table, just out of reach. He groaned, swung his bare feet down and grabbed the bottle, glancing at his watch. Nearly eight-thirty. Had she finished dinner yet? Were they heading to Antonio's place for some hot action?

Who the hell cared? He rolled his eyes and settled back. *Not* going to think about it anymore. Her body belonged to her, she could do whatever the hell she wanted with it.

He grabbed the top of the beer and twisted, then shouted an obscenity, shaking his hand to ease the pain. Damn opener caps. Why the hell didn't she buy twist-offs like any normal person?

He shoved himself up from the couch, slammed his shins against the edge of the table and knocked over the damn flowers.

This time the obscenity was even louder. He raced into the kitchen, grabbed towels and raced back, mopped up the water, propped up broken stems, attempted to rearrange the stupid bouquet into something remotely attractive, then gave up. Forget it. The flowers could look as if they'd been through a disposal and it would suit him just fine.

He sat again, grabbed the crackers, leaned back, feet resting comfortably on the coffee table. Now. Blood. Guts. Death. Misery. Much better. Maybe he could calm the hell down.

He cut himself a hunk of cheese, plopped it on a cracker way too small to hold it, stuffed both into his mouth and followed with more crackers to even the cheese/crunch balance. Looked longingly at his beer, still on the coffee table.

Then remembered he'd forgotten the opener.

To hell with it.

Half a box of crackers and half a brick of cheese later, his throat coated and dry, the movie broke for commercials. Another glance at his watch. Nine-fifteen. If she wasn't home in the next half hour, she and Antonio were going at it for sure.

Not that he gave a flying fellatio.

He reached for the remote, hit the mute button, swung his feet down to get the damn opener, and noticed on the floor a soggy card that must have come with the flowers.

Way past worrying that he was intruding, he flipped it over.

Good friends are worth waiting for. I'm here if you need me. Ben. And a phone number.

"Aw, how special."

His black mood blackened further. He curved his

wrist to chuck the card on the table when he changed his mind. Carried the card and his beer to the kitchen. Retrieved the opener. Opened the beer. Drank half of it, still staring at the card. *I'm here if you need me.*

Laine probably ate that whiny puppy-boy stuff up. Crap.

He took his beer back to the couch, tossed the card onto the coffee table and turned the TV off. Closed the box of crackers. Let his arms rest on his knees and swung the bottle between them. Glanced at his watch again and lowered his head.

He couldn't stand this.

After all this time, he hadn't gotten rid of this stupid—yeah, caveman—feeling that Laine belonged to him. Stupid. Wrong. No longer the case. Once it had been, she'd belonged to him body and soul, and he'd blown it in spades. Now she belonged to herself, and by the end of tonight, her body would belong, however temporarily, to Antonio. Which Grayson undoubtedly deserved, at least in part.

Of course she'd most likely slept with other men while he lived in Chicago. Not as if he thought she should stay pure after he left. But it was entirely different living several states away and dealing with Laine and other men as a concept than sitting here knowing she could be doing one of them right now.

He took a sip of his beer, rubbed his tight forehead, then rested its weight on his palm. She was the reason trying to pick up Candy had seemed stale and predictable. She was why he wanted to mutilate innocent flowers and humiliate this poor Ben guy. He wanted to go to that damn restaurant or to Antonio's place or to wherever Laine was right now, yank her away from him and punch Mr. Pasta all the way back to Italy.

So, what now? What the hell was he left with, if Laine had spoiled him for other women and he couldn't even have her?

Grayson lifted his head and narrowed his eyes into incredulous slits. *What?* What the hell was he saying? Who was the whiny puppy-boy now?

Screw this.

He put the beer down, stalked to the kitchen, got a glass of water, drained it, grabbed an apple from the bowl on her counter and went to dig out his cell phone to check for messages. Moping around feeling sorry for himself wasn't going to accomplish squat.

Two missed calls, the first number was unfamiliar. He dialed into his voice mail and retrieved the message. A deep familiar voice from his past boomed on the line.

"Grayson, Ted Barker. How the hell are you, man? I heard you were at my company today, Omega Source, haven't talked to you in years. You must be back in the city. Give me a call, we need to go and catch up."

Grayson's face broke out into a grin. Holy shit, Ted Barker. His inseparable grade school buddy, they'd grown up practically living at each other's houses in Connecticut—and when not at each other's houses, then they were playing in the country club pool, on the tennis courts or golf course, all on Ted's family membership, of course. No country club time for Grayson's family back then.

The money and big lifestyle change had come right before Grayson had left for Princeton, a year after his father died, when his mom remarried a man appropriately named Rich. Grayson and Ted had lost track of each other during college, but had reconnected when they both took on the City That Never Sleeps after graduation. They'd landed high-paying corporate grunt jobs and had done the twenty-something wild thing pretty thoroughly, until Grayson had moved to Chicago and they lost touch again.

If anyone could interest him in going on a woman hunt, it was Ted. The man could score any phone number he wanted within ten minutes. Grayson couldn't begin to count the number of times he'd bet against Ted and lost. The guy was an artist.

His mood lightened. He'd call Ted tomorrow at work, go out and have a good time with an old friend. This was just the cure he needed at just the time he needed it.

Next message—this number was familiar, one of his clients? He listened, his heart starting to thump with adrenaline. Frank Litman from T. R. Litman and Co. With a project.

Hot damn. Another good sign. He punched off the phone and tucked it back into his briefcase.

Time to regroup. Dispel all negative thinking. Maybe things had gone badly with Mr. Italy. No point assuming Laine was out getting some when he didn't know for sure. Maybe she'd experience the same inhibitor that had kept him from Candy, and she'd end the evening with her Man To Do undone.

He glanced at his watch. Ten minutes more in the half-hour time frame he'd given her to be home score-free.

Okay, here was the deal. If she came back alone, he'd take it as the third sign of the day. And he wouldn't rest until he got her back where she damn well belonged—in bed with him.

A key hit the lock. His heart jumped; he threw

himself on the couch, picked up his beer, turned on the TV again and tried to look indifferent, willing her to come in with only an expression of disgust for company.

The door swung open. Laine walked in, not disgusted, but the next best thing—wary and defiant.

He suppressed a grin and took a swig of beer.

Wary and defiant and alone.

LAINE CLOSED THE DOOR and smiled nonchalantly, keeping a tight grip on the doorknob behind her. Grayson sat on her couch, cradling a beer and watching some horrendous violent movie, surrounded by the remnants of what looked to be a guy-meal of Wheat Thins and cheddar cheese.

This man had been haunting her all evening?

Unfortunately, yes. Like crazy.

She let go of the doorknob and dumped her keys on the worn ''family heirloom'' tray Aunt Barb had given her for graduating college. ''Hi.''

''Hi.'' Grayson got up, put down the beer and moved toward her into the apartment's little entrance-way. He looked relaxed and sexy in gray sweats and an old T-shirt that would probably be incredibly soft to touch. Laine suppressed the urge to lick her lips. Something about the tight, smooth column of a man's hips and waist disappearing under a loose T-shirt hem made her nuts.

''How was your Man To Do?'' He folded his half-bare arms over his chest, projecting every ounce of the smug attitude she knew he'd be wearing.

''The date was awesome, thanks.''

''Uh-huh.'' He glanced at his watch. ''So awesome you're home at nine-thirty.''

"Yeah." She stretched and faked a yawn, realizing too late that the stretch pushed her breasts toward him and lifted the hem of her already high dress.

He put his hands on his hips and tsk-tsked. "What a shame. Hunky Antonio from Italy was a dud."

Laine shrugged. He'd known the second she walked in just by looking at her that she hadn't gotten any. Well, he could think whatever he wanted. No way in hell was she going to tell him Antonio had turned her down. "We didn't hit it off."

He took a step toward her, a teasing light in his eyes. "I'm *really* sorry about that."

Not. The grin he'd tried to suppress wasn't even close to hidden. Worse, another one was trying to curl her own lips to match. *Bad, Laine, bad.* She needed to escape to her room before she gave herself away.

"Wipe that grin off." She smacked him playfully on the shoulder as she walked past. "Smug jerk."

"That's *Mr.* Smug Jerk to you."

Her smile became a laugh. He lunged after her, grabbed her hand and turned her back to face him. "This guy was gross, huh?"

"No."

"Handsome?"

"Very."

"Skinny?"

"Mr. Universe."

"Thuggish, then."

"Charming."

"So?" He pulled to get her to move closer, but she resisted. "What was the problem?"

She sighed mournfully, aware she'd be flirting with disaster, but unable to care enough to stop. "He was a eunuch."

Grayson threw back his head and laughed in real enjoyment, something he did all too rarely. Something that still lit her up with shared pleasure.

"Tony Soprano." He lifted an eyebrow expectantly. "Get it? Antonio—Tony...Eunuch—Soprano."

She grinned. "Very clever."

He pulled harder, enough to make her take a step toward him in the dimly lit hallway, and grabbed her other hand. "So how did he become a eunuch?"

"Oh." She made a face of polite regret. "A bizarre gardening accident."

He laughed again, eyes warm, body language loose, mood playful. He was ten times more dangerous when he let himself relax than when he was trying so hard to get somewhere. "So maybe he wasn't so amazing?"

"I guess not." She sighed and took a step back, stretching their arms nearly horizontal. "He talked about himself the entire evening."

"So?" Predictably he followed with a step forward. "I thought Men To Do was about guys who weren't appropriate for more than one night. Who cares what he talked about?"

Laine's mouth opened, closed. "Oh, well...but..."

"But what? He was handsome, charming, built... what more did you need?"

She bit her lip and looked down at hardwood. No way in hell was she going to say, *He didn't want me.*

"Laine." Grayson's voice went harsh; his grip on her fingers tightened. She looked up into an unexpectedly tense face. "He didn't try anything weird, or try to force you?"

"No." She shook her head, hating the thrill his

protective side brought on. No question if she said yes, Antonio would have ended the evening as a genuine eunuch. "Nothing like that."

"Okay." His tone and features relaxed. "So what, then? What happened to the great Men To Do adventure?"

"It just didn't work out."

"Hmm." He stared at her thoughtfully. "You know what I think?"

Laine rolled her eyes. "No, but I bet you're going to tell me."

"I think maybe you're finally figuring out that nothing can top me." He was blatantly over-cocky, but she was sure to within an inch of her life that if she said, "Oh, yes, Grayson, that's what it is," he'd puff himself up and admit to having known all along.

"I think maybe you're dreaming." She started shuffling slowly away from him, swaying slightly. He followed, one step for every one of hers so that they were doing a strange sexual stalker dance, holding hands in the dim hallway.

"Did he kiss you?"

She shook her head, trying to calculate how soon she could get to the light switch and put an end to the erotic indoor twilight. "No kissing."

"Poor Laine got no action at all, huh."

"Not tonight." Another step back, which he negated by taking another one forward.

"You got all dressed up." His voice dropped to a soft drone; his eyes moved intimately over her body. "All horned up for this hot date, and nothing happened."

"I'm fine." Breathing became harder, as if the air

in the apartment had turned from gas to solid and her lungs couldn't handle the transition.

"I know you." He moved closer, whispering. "Once you get turned on, only one thing can cure it."

"Grayson…"

"Are you going to take care of it yourself?"

"I don't know."

"How? Tell me how."

She swallowed and gave a laugh that sounded forced, because it damn well was. She wasn't horny in the least from the night with Antonio, but ten minutes in Grayson's presence, she was nearly crazed. "That's *my* concern."

His fingers twined in hers; he twisted her arms so they went around her back and brought her within an inch of his body, trapping her hands behind her. She could smell his familiar, sexy smell, and it nearly undid her.

"Give me a hint."

She shook her head, tried to inhale another chunk of air.

"Laine." His voice was still a gruff whisper; his arms were loose around her, but she knew the strength in them, how tightly they could hold her—and how gently. "If you won't let me touch you, at least give me something to think about when I take care of myself tonight."

She closed her eyes. The creep. He was so good. He knew she'd lie awake now, thinking of him thinking of her, imagining him hardening under his own stroking hand. Remembering how she loved to watch him pleasure himself, loved the curious and unusually vulnerable moment when he gave himself over to something other than his extraordinary self-control.

"What are you going to do, Laine?" He murmured the words nearly in her hair; her body responded wildly to his closeness the way it hadn't to Antonio's. One step and she'd be fully in his arms, one step and she'd be pressed against him. She didn't need to look down to know he was getting hard. She knew him that well.

But she also knew she wasn't going to take that step, no matter how tempting. He was tricking, teasing, using all the same old methods that used to work so well, and still would if she weren't stronger now.

Instead she'd show him how strong in the only language he understood. Show him that two could play his twisted game where neither of them would end up satisfied. Show that she was in control of herself now, that she wouldn't give in the second he beckoned, not anymore. This would be her moment.

"First." She opened her eyes. Her voice was low and breathy, even as she tried to steady it. "I'm going to take off my shirt. I'm going to touch my breasts, stroke them, roll my nipples the way you loved to do, pull, pinch—pain, but not too much."

He swallowed, the arms holding her stiffened. "And then…"

"Then I'm going to slide my panties down, one inch at a time until I'm naked and I can feel the room's air between my legs."

"Then—" His voice broke; he cleared his throat. His eyes were burning into hers with such intensity, she had to look down at his chest, rising and falling with his uneven breaths.

"Then I'm going to lie back on the bed and spread my legs."

"God, Laine."

"Spread them wide and touch myself. Two fingers, light circles."

"I know." He was fighting for control. "Two fingers, light circles, I know."

They both swallowed at the same time. The atmosphere changed, equalized. Somehow it wasn't her moment anymore, not totally. Nor his. He wasn't controlling her, she was no longer trying to torture him. Their words had become a sex act without a single caress or erotic touch.

She glanced down at the bulge in his sweats. One step, one reach and she could be holding him, feeling his smooth hardness. Tasting him again.

And then what?

She was finally old enough to ask that question. Finally smart enough to lead with her brain. *And then what?*

"That enough for you?" She disengaged her hands and stepped back, the sudden distance between them like an emotional loss.

He watched her in the hallway; the tension stretched. For a second she was afraid that all he had to say was, "No, that wasn't enough," and she'd cave. But in the next second she knew his pride wouldn't let him. She'd won this round.

His nod confirmed her intuition.

"Terrific." She smiled a supercheery uninvolved smile and turned to walk down the rest of the hall to her room.

"Laine."

She turned back and the supercheery uninvolved

smile dropped off her face. He stood, leaning one arm against the wall as if he needed help to stay upright. His eyes weren't the playful, teasing bedroom eyes he generally wore, nor the cool, calculating eyes of Grayson the Seducer. They were warm, open, slightly tortured—human and fallible. The part of Grayson he almost never let out, which she'd bet she was one of the few people on the planet ever to have seen.

"What?"

"I...want you." He swallowed convulsively. "I want to...be with you again."

Her heart stopped beating, she could swear. She imagined it like a cartoon character who emerges from a ten-thousand-foot drop apparently unscathed, then thousands of crack lines creep over him and he crumbles into a pile of rubble.

"And then what?" She had to force her mouth to form the words.

He blinked. A guarded look, a blank mask started to cover his face again. Laine cringed, not even aware she'd been stupid enough to hope, until that hope took a painful dive back into its black hole.

"I...what do you mean?"

"After we do it." She lifted both arms, let them drop back to her sides. "After we get together and screw each other's brains out like we used to. Then what?"

He gestured with the arm close to the wall and bumped his elbow so hard that she winced. He grunted and grabbed the joint, pain evident on his face, even through all his efforts to suppress it.

And that was it. Suppression. Not letting anything out. Nothing to crack the cool invulnerable exterior.

Even now she knew his mind was spinning wildly,

trying to guess how to answer such a stupid question and still get laid. *And then what?* He was trying not to roll his eyes, trying not to say, *Jeez, you are such a girl! It's so simple, you, me, we do it, what is the problem here?*

She nodded. "That's what I thought."

He looked at her incredulously. "I haven't answered yet."

"I know what you're thinking—'After we do it, then what? Simple! We do it again!' Until you get tired of me and need a break. Then we don't do it. Until you get tired of the break and need me. Then we do it again."

She backed down the hallway and paused outside her door. "Not this time, Grayson. This time I'm looking for a man who plays by *my* rules."

She went into her room, leaving him gaping in the hallway, and closed the door. Sat on her bed, fists clenched, and listened to his footsteps coming down the hall…and into his own room.

Long exhale, then she started her yoga breathing— filling her abdomen, her rib cage, her chest, then letting the air out slowly and evenly, trying to clear her mind.

Her mind would not stay remotely clear. She'd done a good thing tonight, stayed true to what she knew was right, hadn't given in to his tricks or to her deep attraction. She'd put her will of iron to the test and found it strong enough.

But after she relaxed here for a minute or so, then did her sun-salute yoga series, she'd hit NYdates.com and find someone else to be her Man To Do. She hoped to God she'd be luckier this next time with whoever she found, so she'd have a new lover to focus on.

Because she knew down to her toes that at the very next opportunity Grayson was going to try again. And she didn't have to be a blacksmith to know that iron, with enough heat applied, would eventually melt.

6

From: Laine Blackwell
Sent: Friday
To: Angie Keller; Kathy Baker
Subject: My Man To Do

Well, here's the scoop. Antonio said he was from
Italy, but then it turns out he's only from Italy
''in his heart,'' which, as far as I could tell,
means Antonio is full of it. Strike one. Then he
ordered for me, when I hadn't even had the
chance to…

LAINE STOPPED TYPING. The girls weren't going to
care about where he came from or that he ordered for
her. Nor would they care how boring he was. Heck,
she shouldn't care how boring he was. When it came
to a Man To Do, personality was not the issue, as
Grayson had so thoughtfully pointed out last night.

She deleted the entire paragraph.

Okay, date report, get this: he didn't want me!
Turns out Antonio Italian Stud was a good boy
from Brooklyn who thought Laine was Evil Slut
From Hell. He probably went home and beat
himself (off) for the sin of associating with me.

Jeez. I can't even remember the last time a guy turned me down! Not that I'm the ultimate prize, but a guy? Turning sex down? Does this really happen? Seems to me most of them are out for it any which way they can get it.

Anyway, I have already scoped out the next possibility and I have two (count 'em) promising ones. I wrote to the first one and he e-mailed me back right away, definitely sounded interested in getting together. On his profile he reports that he makes $200K per year. Quick jaunt to St. Thomas for a long weekend anyone? Yes, please! Thank you very much! His name is Kevin, but I'll call him the Rich Guy. Second guy I haven't heard from yet, but his name is Joe and his picture shows him in a tank top, looking like Mr. Muscle. His profile was about two sentences long. So I'll call him the Silent Stud. Details to follow once I have some!

Laine

LAINE WALKED INTO Clark's Diner for her usual Saturday lunch date with Judy, relishing the air-conditioned air on her overheated skin. Her head throbbed, her eyes felt swollen and heavy, and someone had stuffed a cantaloupe up into her forehead. Sinus hell. The humidity was building, a heat wave was predicted for a few unbearable days until a thunderstorm would bring the area relief, the usual summer pattern. Days like this she wanted to move to the North Pole.

She lifted her hair, wishing she'd pulled it back off her neck, and searched the crowded colorful booths

and tables until she finally saw Judy waving near the
back of the room.

"I hate this weather." She slid into the booth,
wincing as the part of her thighs not covered by shorts
rubbed over red vinyl that didn't want to let go.

"Me, too." Judy closed the menu she'd been reading and leaned eagerly across the table. "But enough
about that, what's going on with Grayson?"

"Oh, well, not much." She gulped half her glass
of water, and glanced over midgulp to find Judy still
watching her expectantly. Of course, Laine wouldn't
get off that easily. "I mean, he hasn't changed."

"Has he been…you know…" Judy waggled her
eyebrows. "Trying to *reacquaint* the two of you?"

"Sort of. But you know him. He just wants me so
other men can't have me."

"Oooh." Judy rubbed her hands together. "You
told him about Men To Do?"

"Mmm-hmm."

"And?"

Laine shrugged and pinched the bridge of her nose,
wishing someone would invent a sinus Wet-Vac. "He
hates any endeavor that doesn't feature him center
stage."

"Jealous, huh."

"I guess." She tried to sound as if she was dripping with ennui, but it didn't quite work. The ugly
truth? Though she'd never go out of her way to hurt
anyone, deep down, the fact that Grayson was jealous
thrilled her.

Sick. Just plain sick.

"So?" Judy tuned her sharp eyes to Intuition
Mode. "You still have feelings for him?"

Laine inhaled quickly and reached for her water

again. Feelings? Lust, sure. Affection, ditto. Maybe residual pain and bitterness that she hadn't expected. But not feelings the way Judy meant. She couldn't risk that. "Not unless he undergoes a total personality change. Maybe not even then."

"Hmm." Judy frowned thoughtfully. "I still think you guys were made for each other. If you'd just find some way to—"

"Can I take your order, ladies?"

Judy made a sound of frustration and handed her menu over. "Okay, I'll have the chicken breast on focaccia, with fries."

"Chicken soup, please, with extra crackers and a side salad." Laine passed her menu over, unopened, relieved at the chance for a subject change.

This wasn't the time or place to deal with her feelings. She'd woken up uneasy and down, not her usual mood at all, especially not since she quit work. Worse, she was half relieved, half disappointed to find Grayson had left to go home to Princeton. Which unnerved her further. She shouldn't care either way, but on the one hand, her apartment had felt empty and lifeless, and on the other, she'd been glad not to have to build up defenses before coffee.

After coffee she'd been unable to focus. She'd tried practicing her tap routine and practically stepped on her own toes, couldn't concentrate on her French homework, and wasn't even really that jazzed when the e-mail from Kevin came in confirming their date next week.

"So, anyway, this morning I had another e-mail from this Kevin guy I told you about." She paused for another gulp of ice water and pressed her fingers tentatively to her forehead, which felt bruised from her packed sinuses. "He wants to go out next Friday. This one definitely sounds promising."

"Ew, the rich guy?" Judy grimaced as if she'd just swallowed sour milk. "He sounded *horrible.*"

"Not for what *I* need him for."

"Ick."

Laine sighed. Judy would never understand. She was looking for the dream of White Knights and Forever, and nothing else would do. Fine, but limiting in the meantime. Laine was going to make every second of her life count.

She bent her head to dig through her purse for a decongestant, wincing as the movement increased the pressure behind her face.

"Laine, why are you wasting time like this?"

"What, looking for my medicine?"

"This Men To Do stuff."

"It's not wasting time, it's living!" She put heartburn medicine, a Band-Aid and three moist towelette packages on the table and kept digging. "You know, I think I should buy a kick-ass black minidress for this date. One that advertises up front what I want out of the evening. I was probably too demure with Antonio and then shocked the hell out of him by coming right out and asking. Guys want the green light so they can make the moves themselves."

"Laine."

She lifted her head. "What?"

Judy made a face as if Laine had just pulled off her rubber mask to reveal that she was, in fact, Zorgon, Alien Warrior. "You go so far out of your way to justify your own fear, it's incredible."

"Fear?" Laine closed her hand over the sinus medicine. "Fear of what?"

"Commitment."

Laine blinked. This day was getting so weird she was starting to think she should just have stayed in bed. "Huh?"

"You do everything in bits, never stick with anything. Finding a Man To Do is just another symptom."

"Wait a second." Laine popped two tablets into her mouth and swallowed them with the last of her water. "I'm not the one with the commitment issues. That's Grayson's thing. When the time is right, the person is right, I'll settle down. But I'm still young and I have many childbearing years ahead of me. There's no hurry."

Judy's left eyebrow made its patented cynical trip halfway up her forehead. "If you say so."

Laine stared at her incredulously. "What would you—"

"Here you go, ladies." The waitress put down Judy's sandwich and Laine's soup, a huge bowl packed with noodles, chunks of chicken and vegetables, the surface dotted with floating bits of herbs.

"Mmm." Laine inhaled rapturously, hoping as a side benefit the steam would help drain her congestion. "This looks delicious."

"Is that a surprise?" Judy rolled her eyes with good humor. "You *always* have the chicken soup."

"See?" Laine held up her hands in a duh shrug. "I don't have a problem with commitment. Chicken soup and I have been happy for years."

Where she expected Judy to laugh, Judy merely nodded, a polite smile on her face, which made Laine's body flinch in irritation. Commitment issues? What the hell was she talking about? Laine wanted to have fun right now, but when the opportunity and the man presented themselves, she'd commit herself silly.

"So." She leaned her elbows on the table, determined to revitalize their usual easy chatter. "My classes have been awesome so far."

"Remind me what you're taking."

"Yoga, a cooking class, pottery, French, tap dancing…" She counted them off on her fingers. "And I think I'm going to sign up for skydiving, too."

Judy performed an impressive jaw drop. *"Skydiving?"*

"Yeah, wouldn't that be amazing?"

"Getting into a plane and *jumping out?"*

"Uh-huh." Laine accepted a water refill from the waitress. The idea had intrigued her most of her life, though she couldn't ever see herself actually doing it. But! Her summer of fun was the perfect time for that kind of adventure.

"So the woman who won't order anything but chicken soup is going to jump out of an airplane."

Laine rolled her eyes. "It's not quite the same league."

"I guess not." Judy kept her eyes on her silverware, methodically aligning the handles perpendicular to the table edge. Laine suppressed more irritation and dug into her soup. What was up today? Usually she and Judy bounced cheerfully from topic to topic.

"So…is that guy Ben still sending you flowers?"

"Mmm-hmm." Laine nodded, her mouth full of hot noodles.

"What's his deal?"

"He's got scads of money, he's really sweet, gentle, patient, looking for that 'perfect special someone.'

He knows it's not me. I bet my cousin Frank told him to watch out for me. He probably sends the flowers because of that, or just because he's a sweetheart. Grayson thinks he's trying to get laid.'' She rolled her eyes dramatically, trying to suppress a strange twinge of sadness. ''Typical.''

''Oh, wow.'' Judy's eyes shone; she picked up her sandwich. ''Why don't you want Ben? He sounds wonderful.''

''I don't know. I guess the chemistry wasn't right, for one. And the whole time we were on the date, I felt suffocated. Like he never took his eyes off me, never even blinked as far as I could tell. And he wanted to know *everything* about me, wanted me to talk about myself the entire time.''

''What?'' Judy said the word so loudly she looked around to make sure no one was paying attention before she leaned forward and lowered her voice. ''Do you have any idea how few men want to hear women talk about themselves?''

''Yes, I know. But he wasn't right for—'' Laine dropped her spoon, which splashed into her soup and spilled broth on the table. *Hello? Who's calling? Only the obvious.* ''Judy! I'll set Ben up with *you!* I'm serious. You'd probably die for him. He's really adorable, kind of short and round, but totally handsome.''

Judy stopped a French fry halfway to her mouth, and turned bright red. ''I don't think—''

''Forget it.'' Laine held up her hand to stop further objections. ''It's settled. I'll fix you guys up.''

''Oh, I couldn't do that.'' Judy shook her head, then kept on shaking it as if her head-shaking synapses had shorted out. ''Not a blind date, I'd be so nervous.''

"A foursome, then, with Grayson and me." Laine grinned, picturing the four of them at the table. Judy and Ben, her and Grayson, laughing, talking, having a few drinks. God, it would be fun. Like old times. No room for chasing or worries about sex. Just a fun, friendly night out.

"I...I..."

"I'm sorry, who has commitment issues here?" She gestured between herself and Judy. "Who stays home every night and won't go near men?"

Judy wrinkled her nose. "Touché, you bum."

"So?"

"So..." Judy looked around helplessly and hunched her shoulders. "Okay."

"Ha! Excellent!" Laine picked up her spoon and brandished it in triumph. "I'll set it up. Leave everything to me."

She attacked her soup again, headache much better, the pressure behind her eyes diminishing. What an ideal solution. She should have thought of getting Judy and Ben together weeks ago. Laine and Grayson would be the perfect comfortable backdrop for a date like that.

The idea cheered her to the point where, after lunch, she would go shopping for that killer black dress. Wear it on her date with Kevin the Rich Guy and knock him dead.

Oh, yeah. She imagined him, a handsome stranger, eyes lighting up at the sight of her, his strong hands unzipping the zipper, then following its path down her back, warming her skin, turning her to watch the dress slide off her body.

Mmm.

Except when she gazed into his fantasy eyes to invite a kiss, damn it, the eyes that stared back belonged to Grayson.

LAINE SAUNTERED INTO the kitchen, her third trip in the past hour. Five o'clock, she'd gotten very little accomplished, and she was restless and hungry for salt. Or maybe sugar. Or both.

She threw open the cabinet. Peanuts, pretzels, potato chips, Wheat Thins, Triscuits, popcorn, licorice, jelly beans, lollipops, chocolate. What to have, what to have?

Behind her, in the living room, Grayson grunted; she closed her eyes. Her frequent trips to the snack cabinet had *nothing* to do with him working out in her living room. With no shirt on.

Nothing.

For God's sake, the guy was a freaking work of art. He'd been a hunk in his twenties, but his thirties were promising to be even better. He had that solid perfect shape that maturity gives to some men, while taking it away from others.

Drool.

She picked up the package of potato chips, then put it down and picked up the pretzels. The big, thick, sourdough, supercrunchy ones that made your head vibrate when you chewed them.

Giving in to her longing, she leaned on the counter, picked out a pretzel and settled in to watch Grayson do lunges with twenty-pound weights on each shoulder.

"What the hell are you eating, glass?"

She grinned and swallowed. "Pretzel, want one?"

He shook his head, blew out a breath of exertion and changed legs. His muscles bulged and receded with his movements; a drop of perspiration ran down his torso and left a glistening stripe in spite of the air-conditioning.

Mmm. She took another pretzel. Better than TV.

"Nothing better to do than watch me?"

"Plenty."

"Like what?" He finished his set, took the weights off his shoulders and started a series of biceps curls.

"Study French, practice my tap, sign up for another cooking class, maybe explore ice skating lessons…"

"Sounds busy. Better get to it."

"Yeah, well, I'm taking a break." She crunched another bite, watched his biceps contract and didn't feel like doing any of the stuff she was supposed to be filling her summer with.

"How are things at NYdates.com? Any new prospects?"

"One."

"That's it?" He glanced over at her. "Pretty poor showing."

"It's not easy wading through the weirdos and con artists. I swear half their profiles are crap."

"Meaning?"

"'I like to take long walks and go camping and cuddle by the fire and give hour-long backrubs.' Ha! You know damn well in reality they sit on their asses and flick the channel changer."

He rolled his eyes. "Guys are pigs, is that it?"

"What the hell kind of self-respecting man uses the word *cuddle* in public?"

"One trying to get laid."

"Be serious."

"I am serious. We're programmed to get the female of the species in the sack. We can't help it."

He finished his biceps curls, grabbed a towel from the couch and mopped his face. "It's all about the chase."

The pretzel Laine had just swallowed hit the bottom of her stomach with a thud. She knew this. She knew he thought that way. Why was she letting it upset her? "Right."

"Women do it, too. I bet you don't see many ads that read, 'Moody bitch seeks man to support her in style while she makes him feel inadequate.'"

"No." She held her pretzel and flicked off flakes of salt with her thumbnail. "I guess not."

"Hey." He walked toward her and stopped on the other side of the counter. "I'm kidding. What's the matter?"

"Nothing." She managed a smile.

"Okay." He watched her for a second, then threw the towel around his neck and grabbed a pretzel. "I'm going to take a shower."

He moved down the hallway, crunching, and a minute later Laine heard the water running in the tub.

She closed the bag of pretzels and put it back in her cupboard. Went back to her room. Sat at her computer and stared at her morphing-shapes screen saver.

Okay. Grayson's comment hurt. And she didn't want it to hurt. She didn't want anything about Grayson ever to hurt again.

Worse, if he could still make her feel this way, she needed to dig down and 'fess up to the truth. She didn't want it to be all about the chase between her and Grayson. She wanted to be more than that to him. Something lasting. Even just a friend, and maybe that was what would work best now, in their third incarnation together—first, hot and heavy steadies in college; second, hot and heavy once in a while after graduation; now this, whatever this was.

If they were just friends, Grayson wouldn't be trying constantly to get her into bed. There would be nothing for him to hunt; she'd be a permanent platonic fixture in his life, so they could be open and honest and uncomplicated together.

It was just that being friends was a trifle difficult when every time she was around him she wanted to maul him sexually. On the floor. In the shower. Against the wall. Even on the bed.

She thudded her elbows on her computer desk and covered her face with her hands. Oh, jeez, she had to stop thinking about him that way. In fact, it would be 1smart to stop thinking about him altogether.

She lifted her head; her elbow bumped the mouse, and she grabbed it and clicked to open her e-mail.

From: Angie Keller
Sent: Monday
To: Laine Blackwell; Kathy Baker
Subject: Kevin the Rich Guy

Hey, babycakes, this Rich Guy sounds tree-mendous! Yes, I think I could handle a weekend in St. Thomas just fine, so if he doesn't work out, send him on down to Mama Angie, you hear?

But—and don't take this the wrong way—I've heard diddly-squat about this Grayson character. What gives? You hiding something, girlfriend? Just a hunch. I don't ask much, just to know every little thing about your private life.

But back to the Rich Guy, let us know how it

goes on Friday and here's hoping he's the one! You must be so fired up!

   God bless,
   Angie

Laine closed the e-mail and the program. Yeah. Fired up.

She *should* be fired up. She managed to get that way a lot of the time. Just not right now.

"Git yer ice-cold soda heah." Grayson's imitation of a ballpark vendor made her jump.

She turned, flustered to see him walking toward her holding two cans of Diet Sprite, that same watchful look in his eyes that gave no clue as to what was actually going on in his brain.

He was making her incredibly nervous.

She stood, feeling strangely vulnerable sitting. "Good shower?"

"Yeah." His hair was dark, damp and tousled from toweling. He'd put on shorts and a T-shirt, and looked so good she wanted to cry. "So what's going on?"

"Nothing." She gestured awkwardly to the computer. "I was just on e-mail."

"With your Man To Do?"

"No." She registered the hint of bitterness in his voice and got even more nervous. "With girlfriends."

He took a step toward her; she could smell the fresh-showered smell of his soap—a brand he must have brought with him. There was very little on the planet sexier than soap that smelled as good as after-shave.

He clinked his can to hers. "Here's to old times."

She nodded, hating the melting warmth kicking in

at the thought of what he'd been to her. "And new ones."

He nodded, drank and rested the can on her bookshelf. "How do you want those new times to be, Laine?"

"Friendly." She gestured nervously with her drink. "We should be friends."

"You think that will work."

"Well, yes. I mean, I'm going to get involved with someone else."

"I thought the point of a Man To Do was that you weren't going to get involved."

"No. But I will be sleeping with him, so—"

"So since you'll be sleeping with someone else, you and I get to be friends."

"That's right." She nodded extremely earnestly, then stopped when she realized her extreme earnestness betrayed her nerves. "We get to be friends."

He leaned forward until his face was an inch from hers and she could see the moisture the Sprite had left on his lips. "You know what that is?"

"What?"

"Bullshit."

"Grayson…" She moved back.

"Go ahead, move away. The wall is about a foot behind you, I'll just wait.

She plonked her can on her computer desk, shot her hands to her hips and stood her ground. Damn it, this cat-and-mouse thing had to stop.

She lifted her chin and looked straight into his eyes, daring him to actually verbalize some hint of what he was getting at. "How do *you* want us to go?"

He moved suddenly, catching her completely off

guard, lifted her, swung her around, pushed her back onto the bed, lunged and covered her with his body.

"Like this."

"No way, Grayson. We've been through this." She tried to roll to one side, but he grabbed her wrists and pinned them above her head. She writhed in protest, then realized she was pushing her hips against him, realized he was getting very hard, very fast, and realized that his much-too-tempting bulge was positioned exactly where it could make her lose control. "Get off."

"I'm trying."

"Grayson…" She was not in the mood for his humor.

"Laine…"

"Let me go."

"No." He whispered the word, bent his head, kissed the side of her neck—her second favorite place—then moved up toward her jaw using gentle, slow kisses. The ones he knew made her dreamy and hot and more than willing.

Her breath came faster; she moved again, instinctively wanting to struggle. He pressed down in response, then started a gentle rocking that pushed his erection against her sex and made her fight a moan rising in her throat.

Oh, oh, oh, she was in so much trouble.

He moved his head down farther, still holding her wrists tightly, and caught her nipple between his teeth, through the fabric of her shirt.

She cried out in protest and pleasure, turned on out of her mind.

"I know you. I know you like pain, just a little, not too much. I know the line, how much to give you, when to stop. What other guy is going to do that for you?''

She held herself stiffly, while every atom in her being was pressuring her hips to answer his movements.

"Spread for me, Laine." He kissed her jaw, under her ear, then flicked his tongue gently over her skin in the same spot he'd just kissed. "Let me in."

She shook her head. He had the strength to spread her himself, but he wanted her surrender. She wasn't going to give him that. She still had no answer for her question, *And then what?* She wouldn't give in without it.

"Is this all about the chase, Grayson?"

He stopped moving. Lifted his upper body off her, screwed up his eyes incredulously. "What?"

"I want to know. Is this your gender's preprogrammed need to get laid?''

"How could you—"

"Spare me the outrage. Just answer."

"It's…no. I want you. I always have. I…probably always will."

She felt her body turning off, cooling down. Sure, he wanted her. Wanted some pussy and to hell with who she was or what she felt. He hadn't even kissed her on the mouth, hadn't said anything emotional, just tried to persuade her to spread her legs like a horny teenager attempting his first score.

Damn him all to hell.

He couldn't win this way. She couldn't outwrestle him physically, so she searched for whatever weapon she could use to increase the distance between them.

"Why did you cheat on me in college?"

"*What?*" He rolled off her, sat on the bed. "Jeez,

Laine, that was years ago. I don't even remember. Why the hell do you want to ask me that now?''

''Because you haven't ever answered.''

''How many times are you going to beat me up about this?''

''As many times as it takes until you tell me.''

''Tell you what? I screwed up. I was twenty-two, for God's sake. I was young, I was drunk, I was stupid. End of story. Are you telling me ten years later, you're still angry?''

''I just want to understand it.''

''*I* don't even understand it. How am I supposed to explain it to you? It was just a stupid guy thing.'' He stood, went to retrieve his soda and drank, not as if he enjoyed the taste or was thirsty, but as if he was trying to drown in it. ''Why do you always make things so damn complicated? I want you. Like crazy. You want me just as much. But you persist in trying to go out and screw complete strangers when your perfect Man To Do is right here.''

Ha! That was a laugh. She sat up, pulled her knees to her chest and wrapped her arms around them. ''There's no way you could be a Man To Do.''

''Why?''

''Because we go back a long way. Men To Do are supposed to be strangers. Men you don't care about. Men you can use and say goodbye to and not feel anything more than grateful and happy and well-laid.''

''Right.'' He gave a humorless smile. ''What's the real reason?''

''What do you mean by that?''

''What are you protecting yourself from?''

''Excuse me?'' What the hell was he talking about?

"*Now* who's complicating things? Men can go out and get laid and they're studs, but women have to have some underlying psychological defect that needs analyzing?"

"Okay." He held up his hands in surrender. "You believe what you want. Just answer this. Do you want me?"

She opened her mouth and closed it. God, yes. And he knew it. But this was just another game, another tactic, another way to win. If she admitted it, she'd lost. He'd be relentless, wouldn't stop at anything until they were lovers again. The only way she could stay safe and in control was to resist.

"I'm not going to sleep with you."

"I'm not asking if you are going to sleep with me, I'm asking if you want me."

"You're splitting hairs."

"Okay, I'll answer for you. Because I know you, I know how you look and act and feel when you're turned on, and your body still lights up around me. You want me, but because of these rules, you're not going to let yourself have what you want. How stupid and self-defeating is that?"

"It's not stupid, trust me. It's brilliant."

"You want to explain that?"

She gazed at him, at his handsome face still flushed from the warmth of his exercise and the shower, at his eyes, dark and shooting sparks, and she knew she wasn't going to answer. Not now, not ever. Because the rules of Men To Do and her summer of fun were to keep things light, breezy and don't-look-back uninvolved.

And there was no way she could sleep with Grayson and not get her heart tangled up in him all over again.

7

GRAYSON STRODE INTO the large bar/dining area of the Park Avenue Country Club restaurant, searching the white-cloth-covered tables for a sight of his friend, Ted. Pretty useless activity, considering in all the years he'd known him, Ted hadn't been on time once.

Grayson needed this guy evening for more reasons than just social ones. Jake Farley, the Marketing V.P. from Omega Source had called to say his company was "postponing its decision." He'd bet a million their internal I.T. department had taken the ideas from Jameson's design study and planned to run with them. Happened all the time. "We'll call you" was generally the kiss of death.

Some things you couldn't control. He'd played this sale right all the way down the line, from the initial contact to the proposal stage. Given the client everything it wanted, shown not only how much more it could accomplish in the market, but exactly how Jameson could make it all happen.

A woman brushed by him who looked a little like Laine. His heart leaped, then settled. Speaking of things he couldn't control… He thought he'd given Laine what she wanted, too, all the way down the line. Two days ago when she was watching him work out in her living room, it hadn't taken a mind reader to know she'd been imagining exercise of a very different nature. When he responded, she turned a one-eighty and rejected him. No, he couldn't be her Man To Do for this reason and that one, yadda yadda.

He was starting to think this idea of living with her was going to kill him. When she'd come home from that date with the Italian guy last week, when Grayson had accosted her in the hallway, jealous as hell and trying to make her want *him* for the obvious testosterone-laden reason, he'd suddenly realized he wanted her back. Not only for territorial reasons and not only for sex, but for everything, the way they'd been in college—inseparable, passionate and good friends to boot. Easy and natural, without rules and barriers and baggage. He missed the way they laughed so hard at so much, he missed going out with her to share ethnic food, he missed the way they worked out together, the way their energetic, passionate personalities meshed so well.

Hell, he missed waking up and knowing she was in the world for him the same way he was in the world for her, that extraordinary connection that kept them going through so much crap.

But damned if he knew how to get her to come around. Grayson the Consummate Salesman was striking out on all fronts. How did you get nostalgic and romantic with a girl who wouldn't let you near her?

He needed this evening with Ted in a big way. Not that Ted was one to give advice on relationships, considering his own tended to be calculated in hours. Ted wouldn't remotely understand all this rumination. He'd tell Grayson to grow some balls and go out hunting for new game, and how about them Yankees? Which was just what the doctor ordered tonight—

getting away from frustration and dead ends and shooting the shit with an old buddy.

"Grayson, my man." A large hand slapped him on the back.

He turned, grinning, and grabbed the shorter man in a hug—a manly one, of course.

"Hey, Ted." Grayson pulled back and grinned harder. Ted was a little softer in the face, thicker around the middle, thinner on top, but essentially the same. It was damn good to see him.

"Come on over." Ted gestured to the other side of the room. "I have a table, already ordered us some 'tinis. You still drink 'em, don't you?"

"You bet." Grayson followed him past the huge orange-red bar to a small table and pulled out the wooden chair to sit.

"You look good, man, haven't changed at all." Ted sat, leaned back and slapped his belly. "Haven't put on the married man's pounds like the rest of us, eh?"

Huh? Grayson hoped his face registered polite, pleasant surprise instead of bone-jarring shock. He couldn't imagine Ted staying faithful to one woman for his entire life. He wasn't sure Ted had ever stayed faithful to one woman for an entire week. "You're married? How the hell did that happen?"

The waitress brought their martinis, liberally gifted with olives and onions, the way Ted loved them, straight up and filled to the rim. Ted lifted his in a toast to the waitress. "Thanks, Sarah, love. You're the best. If I weren't married already, I'd ask you."

The waitress rolled her eyes and blushed. "Yeah, I bet you say that to all the girls."

"As a matter of fact, I do."

She laughed and shifted her tray to shoulder height. "Anything more I can get you, let me know."

"Thanks, Sarah." He watched her walk away, her hips swaying attractively under a short black skirt.

Grayson grinned, shaking his head. "You still have it, huh."

"What? What do you mean?"

"Women."

"Oh, that. Whatever. I do it out of habit. They don't take it seriously, neither do I." He reached his drink across the table in another toast, dark eyes brimming with his familiar brand of mischief. "Here's to the former terrors of New York City nightlife finding each other once again."

"Amen to that." Grayson clinked and took his first perfectly chilled sip. "May we live to terrorize again."

"Heck, no." Ted gulped a healthy mouthful and sighed in contentment. "I'm a reformed chicko-holic."

"No kidding. So what's with that, your wife have a gun?"

Ted shook his head gravely. "Something infinitely more powerful than weaponry."

Grayson readied a chuckle. He couldn't wait to hear this. "What's that?"

"My heart, man." He pounded a fist to his barrel chest. "The woman nailed me at first glance. All it takes to stop me going anywhere else is the memory of how she looked the first day I saw her."

Grayson's readied chuckle died. "Be serious."

"I am. Deadly."

Grayson took another sip of his martini. A large one. This was *Ted?*

"Look." Ted dug in his pocket, pulled a snapshot out of his wallet. "Wife and kids. House in Hoboken. Daddy commutes, Mom drives a minivan. Can you believe this?"

"No." Grayson took the photo. What kind of woman would have caused this much of a change in Ted? Angelina Jolie's twin?

A woman of average build, average attractiveness, stood in front of a modest-looking house, two blond boys clinging to her legs. Not Angelina, but her face was intelligent, appealing, and a dynamite smile lit up her features so she glowed, even on camera.

"She's nice-looking." He stared at the photo, feeling a strange twinge of sadness, trying to absorb the fact that Ted, the greatest womanizer New York had ever known, was married. "Cute kids."

"Yeah, they're pretty cool." He beamed to accompany the obvious understatement, accepted the picture back and put it in his wallet. "So what's been going on with you, man? No I-do action for you?"

"I've only been back in the city a few months. I started an interactive media company with a friend from Princeton and I've been trying to make it go. Not much time for anything else."

"Then make time, my friend. Life is too short. What about that woman you couldn't ever get over—Laine."

Grayson grabbed a pick and tried to spear an onion in his drink. "She's fine. I'm using her place to crash when I'm in the city."

"Yea-a-a-h?" Ted dragged the word out patiently, obviously not buying that the story was over. "So what's that like?"

Grayson shrugged, keeping his eyes on the evasive onion. "It is what it is."

"Ha!" Ted smacked his palm on the table between them. "She's still got you. I knew she was It."

Grayson gritted his teeth and stabbed at the onion again. "She doesn't *have* me."

"Sure she does." Ted took another sip of his drink and exhaled blissfully. "So what's the trouble, she's keeping you out?"

"Yes." His mouth snapped shut after the word. This was not the conversation he wanted to be having with Ted. They were supposed to be regaling each other with sordid stories of the old days, ogling women, betting on the Yankees' chances. Taking Grayson away from his troubles, not leading him to them and making him think.

"I can't believe that. You guys were so hot for each other. That kind of thing doesn't change."

"It hasn't changed. She just won't."

"Why?"

"She has a reason, I'm just not convinced it's the real one."

"Hmm. What did you tell her?"

Grayson lifted his head from trying to impale pickled vegetables. What had he told her?

Oh, no.

The words hadn't even exited his mouth and he could already hear how stupid they sounded. *He wanted her.* Is that all he'd managed to communicate? "I told her I wanted her."

"Oh, Gray." Ted puckered as if his drink had turned bitter on him. "I guarantee she *knows* you want her. But if that's all you said, you're screwed, and not the way you want to be. With your history, she's probably afraid of going back to being the on-again, off-again girlfriend.''

Grayson groaned and spanned his temples with one hand, squeezing as if he could get his brain to work better. She probably thought he was the same kind of dick-driven idiot she complained about on NYdates.com.

Is this all about the chase? And then what? He'd heard her questions, but hadn't really listened. Truth to tell, he hadn't been thinking past the moment much himself, had only been aware of how much he missed her, how much he wanted her back in his life.

He just hadn't happened to mention it.

But how the hell could he put himself out there like that, all his feelings on the table, with her running around trying to screw every guy in the city?

''Uh-oh. Someone's still got it bad.''

Grayson shot Ted a warning glance.

Ted leaned forward and set down his drink. ''Let me tell you how it was with Nora. I told you how she made me nuts the first time I saw her. Even then, I knew she was something different. But I didn't know how to approach her any way other than my usual. So I came on to her, same ol', same ol', and guess what?''

''Your first strikeout in history.''

Ted put on a look of mock disgust. ''Thanks. I think.''

''So…what did you have to do?'' The question came out unwillingly, past teeth that wanted to clench. He felt like a wet-behind-the-ears teenager begging older, more experienced boys for tidbits of advice.

''I had to woo her. Yes.'' He held up his hand as

Grayson started to smile. "I said *woo*. The painfully slow, get-to-know-her-first, old-fashioned way."

"You're kidding me. *You* did that?"

"Yup. Flowers, love letters, endless kiss-at-the-door dates. I had blue balls for two months before she finally trusted me."

"Ouch." Grayson winced and pressed his legs together.

"Yeah, it's worse than that. I had to spend time 'discussing the relationship.' I had to admit to having flaws and agree to work on them." He shuddered. "I can't really talk about it."

Grayson started to laugh midsip, choked and pounded himself on the chest. "God, what a nightmare."

Ted grinned. "Men are by far the inferior gender."

"Until the sink clogs, then we're indispensable."

"Right." Ted laughed and scrubbed his hand through his once-thick, wavy hair. "I'd do it all again. She's an amazing woman."

Grayson nodded, alcohol invading his cells, doing that dangerous mushy thing to his brain. That thing that made strong, aggressive men feel gooey, passionate feelings and want to verbalize them. Maybe he'd been thinking too much with his dick and hadn't gone about this the right way at all. Yeah, she'd rejected him, but maybe it wasn't all about Men To Do. Maybe she wanted some assurance that he wasn't going to treat her like dirt all over again.

Gee, Grayson, ya think?

He tried to spear the onion again, but the little bugger slipped away, probably snickering by now. "That would explain the non-laughter when I joked that for men it was all about the chase."

"Bingo." Ted stuck his pick into his drink and came up with the onion on the first try. "You have to convince her you're serious. But first, my man, you have to be sure you are serious. They can smell an ounce of bullshit a mile away. Laine's a terrific woman and she doesn't deserve bullshit."

Grayson gave up his onion-spearing campaign and settled for another sip, disguising a grimace as the salt/pickle flavor began to interfere with the gin. Was Ted serious? Grayson's track record with Laine sucked; he'd gotten bored with Meg in Chicago after a couple of years. Apart from a few more warm fuzzies recently than he was used to feeling, how could he be sure? How could he be sure that he wouldn't— God forbid—hurt her again? He couldn't stand that.

But what if it really was all about the chase for him?

"How did you...know with Nora?" His voice came out thick with embarrassment. If Ted made fun of him, he'd be forced to start punching.

"You're a goner, Gray." Ted's voice was mercifully free from teasing. If anything, he sounded respectful.

Grayson relaxed his fist. "I guess."

"You guys were made for each other. Anyone around you knew it. You lit each other up."

"We still do."

"Nora and I have that. I've seen this woman at her absolute bitchy, moody worst, when she's looking like hell warmed over, and she still lights me up. And she's seen me at my most neglectful, bad-tempered, unshowered, morning-breath worst, too, and still insists I'm a god descended to earth. So that's one way you know."

Ted drained his martini, signaled Sarah for two more without asking Grayson, his usual habit, which was the reason Grayson had spent most of his nights out with Ted in a drunken blur. "And another thing. It sounds simplistic, but she mattered. I felt if she turned me down, if I lost her, then that was it for me, I'd never find anything like that again. She was worth crawling to, man, and I was not a crawling kind of guy. I used to figure if a woman didn't want me, screw 'er, there were plenty more who would. But after I met Nora, other women didn't interest me. I mean, hell, I'm not dead, I still look. But now I stop before I leap, and I think about whether the thrill would be worth losing her. I'm telling you, it never even comes close."

Grayson grabbed the pick, feeling buzzed and on high-alert mentally, as if someone had poured extra-caffeinated soda down him along with the booze. In a tremendous *oh, yeah* moment, Ted was putting words to emotions he was only barely aware he felt. If Laine went out and found a Man To Do, it would break him. He'd have to move out; there was no way he could stand by and watch that crap. Then there was the night a week or so ago at Proof, when Ms. Lorena/Candy had practically thrown herself at him and he couldn't fathom being with anyone but Laine.

He did have it bad. Now he just had to find a way to let Laine know.

He stabbed the pick into his drink and shocked the hell out of himself by coming up with both the onion and the olive.

Even if it meant blue balls.

From: Laine Blackwell
Sent: Thursday
To: Angie Keller; Kathy Baker
Subject: Next MTD!

I'm on my way to dinner with Kevin the Rich Guy. And I have a date with Joe the Vain Stud next week if this one doesn't work. Wish me luck. Here's hoping by the end of the night I will be one happy and satiated puppy.

Laine reread what she had written. Fine, but sounded less than enthusiastic. She deleted the paragraph and moved her cursor back to the beginning.

I'm on my way to dinner with Kevin the Rich Guy! And (dramatic pause) I have a date with Joe the Silent Stud next week if this one doesn't work. Woohoo, an embarrassment of testosterone riches. Wish me luck!!!

That was better.

Oh, and Angie, you asked why I was being so quiet about Grayson. Not much to say, that's why. He keeps trying to get into my pants, but you'd be proud of me. I keep those suckers zipped. He doesn't remotely count as a Man To Do, and I'm standing tall on that point. Didn't even tell him about my date tonight.

A credit to the fine institution of casual sex am I.

Bowing gracefully,

Laine

"SORRY. Excuse me, Laine." Kevin turned his chair slightly away to answer his cell phone for the second time during their meal at Wild Ginger Restaurant. "Hello? Yeah. Uh-huh. God, he's a bastard. Okay. Do what you need to. Right. Not enough capital there. Okay."

Laine brought another forkful of Pad Thai noodles to her mouth, loving the combination of spicy, salty, sweet-and-sour flavors. Chili, fish sauce, palm sugar and tamarind. She and Grayson used to call this dish Desert Island Food. The one they'd pick for all eternity.

She took a sip of Singha beer and stared longingly at Kevin's red curry with duck. Another favorite of hers. But apparently Kevin wasn't into sharing. What was the point of eating at a restaurant that served family style if you couldn't dig into whatever appealed? She and Grayson would sometimes order more food than they could possibly eat, just to have an array of flavors and textures on one plate. Then they'd bag it all up and eat it the next day, sometimes cold right out of the container, sitting in their underwear watching old movies in bed.

"Sorry about that." Kevin slipped the tiny phone back into his shirt pocket. "Now, where were we?"

She didn't know where he was, but *she* was having way too many trips down Grayson Memory Lane recently. Times together she hadn't thought about in years. Good ones, too, not just the bad. Including what they'd done in this restaurant last time they'd been here...

"You were telling me about your ex-wife not appreciating you." She tried to put a tinge of polite sarcasm in the phrase, to send the message that maybe this wasn't appropriate get-to-know-you conversation.

"Oh, yeah. The laundry thing. So this one time I was in a huge hurry, had a few shirts I needed clean, you know?"

He looked expectant. Laine nodded, her mouth full of Pad Thai. Shirts he needed clean. Yes, she knew.

"So I take them down to the basement, thinking I'm being a nice guy not asking her to do them. I put them in the washer, turn it on, do the whole damn thing myself. And is she grateful?"

Now there was a no-brainer. Laine shook her head. No, she wasn't grateful.

"She *screams* at me. 'Didn't I see the huge pile of dirty laundry down there and would it have been so hard to add a few things to spare her some work,' blahblahblah. Like I didn't help enough. You know?"

Laine speared more noodles and nodded. Yes, Kevin, she knew.

He went on. Since listening didn't interest her, she watched him while he talked. He was very attractive. Dark hair that did all the right curling wavy things over his forehead. Dark eyes that jumped out of his face. Impressive build. Square, clean-shaven jaw.

If only his square, clean-shaven jaw would close and stay that way. If only he'd discuss some topic other than money and his ex. Damn, this was depressing. One thing she and Grayson had always been able to do was talk. Not about emotional things, not about the relationship—he wasn't wired for that, and that silence had ultimately killed them.

But everything else had been fair game and they'd talked about it all. Well, okay, a lot of the time they talked about sex. Oh God, they talked about sex.

Sometimes she'd be ready to come just from a conversation. He'd tease her, tell her everything he wanted to do to her, share his fantasies, stuff he'd done that turned him on and stuff he'd never do that turned him on, and all of it got her hot.

She finished the last bite of Pad Thai her stomach would hold in its current upset state. Kevin was still dragging his ex through the coals, gesturing, nurturing his own outrage, lost and needy, covering it with bluster.

What was she doing here?

Immediately she chided herself for the moment of weakness, reached for her beer and took another fortifying gulp. She knew exactly what she was doing here. Enjoying herself. Fulfilling her promise for the summer.

Grayson was out tonight with Ted, the most predatory male she'd ever known, but also one of the most charming and fun. No doubt Ted was leading Grayson into an adventure or two involving other women. No doubt Grayson would go eagerly, if only to salve his wounded pride after her rejection. So he was out trying to get laid because she'd blown him off, and she was trying to get laid to keep him at a distance. God, how sad.

She sighed. Well, she wasn't trying to get laid tonight. Not anymore. Probably hadn't even planned to when the evening started, if she'd admit it. She hadn't felt like wearing the black mini do-me dress that still hung in her closet. Maybe on her date next week with Joe…if she could stand another one of these tortured occasions.

The waiter pointed to her beer and raised his eyebrows in question, so as not to interrupt the latest saga of Ann the Ex. Laine shook her head. No more beer. She didn't want to drown her logic or her resolve in alcohol.

The way she and Grayson played these mind games was ridiculous. Childish. But for some reason when they got together, they could never get past the damaging patterns, never bridge the communication gap far enough to have a healthy relationship. Maybe they were too passionate together, maybe the sexual chemistry was just too hot. She wished it had faded a long time ago so they could at least be buddies.

Kevin stopped his tirade long enough to shovel three forkfuls of curry into his mouth, chew loudly, swallow and continue.

"Anyway, that's ancient history. So what about you?"

Laine blinked in surprise. She'd set herself on auto-listen and hadn't anticipated being required to provide any of the conversation.

"Oh, well, I'm going to Columbia journalism school in the fall." Which seemed so far away as to be totally unreal. "And this summer I'm taking a variety of courses to—"

"My ex-wife took a course the summer before she left me." Kevin started fiddling with the label on his beer. "I think it was on feminist literature or something. She met her boyfriend there. I don't know if she was cheating on me, but she started showing up with him about two weeks after she moved out. Doesn't take a genius to put those pieces together. Guy's a total jerk, too. So what if he does laundry if he's a jerk, you know?"

He looked so genuinely miserable, Laine actually summoned a fair amount of sympathy. Kevin probably was an okay guy. Maybe insensitive, but hey, he didn't have a lock-up on that trait. Maybe some serious anger hanging around, but she'd bet it stemmed from the fact that he still loved his wife like crazy. He certainly wasn't here to get to know Laine.

"Why don't you call her, Kevin? Maybe this new guy is just a way of acting out. Making you stop and pay attention to what's really important. Maybe deep down she's hoping you can change, that you guys can find a way back to each other, to fix what went wrong the first time and try again. Because if the emotion is still there, if it's still deep and compelling, then it's got to be worth fighting to build the communication and the…trust…that will…"

Something in her brain knocked and started trying to send some pretty loud signals. She locked the door and tossed the key. No way.

She took a deep breath. "All I'm saying is that…maybe you should just invite her to the movies."

He shook his head. "She won't go."

"Have you tried? Have you done anything but stay away and assume defeat?"

Her eyeballs froze, lids wide. Okay, if she continued this conversation any longer she was officially going to freak herself the hell out. End. Finished. No more. Not until she could get home alone and think through what she'd just said.

The waiter cleared their plates; they refused dessert. Kevin let her pay her half, and they walked out onto Grove Street into the soft night air and city smells, toward Bleecker Street and the Christopher Street subway stop.

"I know it's early, but think I'll call it a night."

Kevin scratched the back of his neck. "I'm sorry I went on and on about Ann. To be honest, I don't really think I'm ready for this dating thing yet. I can't deal with the thought of starting from scratch with someone else when she and I fit so well together. You know? I mean if things were totally dead between us it would be easy to move on, but there's still something…"

"I know what you mean."

"You do?" He craned his head around and peered at her expression.

"Yeah." For a second she was afraid she was going to cry.

"I was part of the problem, too." He made a hopeless gesture and let his hand fall back to his side. "I couldn't talk to her the way she wanted. I couldn't say the stuff she wanted me to say. Half the time I didn't even know what it was she wanted to hear. And she never told me. But she won't stop being furious at me just because I couldn't read her mind. You know?"

Laine stared at him in horror. Oh God. She knew.

He caught her expression and laughed without humor. "I'm sorry, you must think I'm a complete loser."

"No." She put a hand on his arm. "Not at all. What you just said…hit a nerve. That's all."

"Oh. Okay. Well, sorry again. You seem like a really nice woman. I hope you find what you want."

I don't even think I know what I want.

She forced a smile. "Maybe Ann will take you back if you try again. If this guy she's with really is a jerk."

"Maybe. She wanted me to go to counseling. I said

I'd rather die, but maybe it's worth it. Because being without her feels like death."

Laine stood on tiptoes and kissed him on the cheek. "Tell her that, Kevin. Just tell her that."

He nodded awkwardly. "Yeah, okay. So, um, can I walk you to the subway?"

"No, no." She pointed at the entrance across the street. "It's right there."

"Oh. Right. Sorry." He laughed nervously and started down the block, obviously eager to get the evening over with.

"Good night." She crossed the street and went down into the hot, stale-smelling air of the underground tunnel. Thank God, Grayson wasn't going to be home yet—if he even made it back tonight. He and Ted were always out most of the night. She needed to sit down and to think this through without his distracting presence.

What Kevin had said had turned everything upside down. Because right now she was on the verge of admitting that she really didn't want a Man To Do.

She wanted Grayson.

8

LAINE LET HERSELF INTO the apartment, dropped her keys on Aunt Barb's sorry excuse for a family heirloom, kicked off her black flats and dragged herself down the hallway toward her room. God, she was exhausted. Having to spend the evening attentive to and interested in someone who neither caught her attention nor interested her was draining—no offense to Kevin. Not to mention all these weird and disturbing thoughts that had popped into her head regarding Grayson. When Kevin talked about how his ex blamed him for not being able to read her mind, the proverbial lightbulb had switched on in Laine's head. Had she ever sat down and talked to Grayson about the failings in their relationship, or about her fears of how she'd be treated if they resumed it?

Nope.

And thank God she didn't have to at the moment. She just wanted to change out of her dress, put on shorts and a ratty T-shirt and watch—

"Hi."

She lurched to one side at the sound of his voice and put a hand to her chest. "Jeez, Grayson, you scared me to death."

"Sorry."

She got her heartbeat under control and stood facing him in the doorway to his room. Something was up with him. He looked subdued, wary.

"I didn't think you'd be back this early." She arched a teasing eyebrow, feeling pain jab at her stomach. "Or at all. Ted losing his touch?"

"Ted's married."

"Married?" Laine clutched her throat and pretended to have trouble breathing. *"Ted?* What sins did this woman commit to deserve him?"

"He's given up the hunt. House in the 'burbs, kids, the whole marital enchilada." He rubbed the back of his head.

"Go figure." Something was definitely bothering him, she knew the signs. And she'd learned not to bother asking. He'd never admit anything was wrong.

"Where were *you?* On another Men To Do date?"

She squelched the instinct to deny it. He might as well know. "Yeah."

He folded his arms across his T-shirted chest. "Then I didn't think you'd be home this early, either."

She shrugged. "This guy didn't work out. He was hung up on his ex. Talked about their problems the entire evening. I think he wasn't really ready to date yet. Not really interested in anything but her. So I was just—" She snapped her jaw closed. *Shut up, Laine. You're way overexplaining.* "So…you had fun?"

"Yeah. It was really good to see him."

"Good." She felt the next question forming on her lips before her brain could stop it. "Did the married version of Ted still provide you with prospects?"

"I wasn't interested in any."

Laine blinked. He wasn't?

He reached out and touched her hair, pushed a lock back off her temple, eyes warm. "Seems to me getting laid shouldn't be this hard, Laine. For either of us. What's that all about, do you think?"

"I don't know." She found herself whispering, using all her might not to stare at him with the longing she felt. Images and memories of him and of them had been with her all evening, and the discovery that he hadn't been interested in anyone else had weakened her resolve even more. Made her think maybe he wasn't interested in other women because no one could take Laine's place, the same way no one seemed to be able to take his.

Damn it. She was doing it again. Projecting *her* feelings onto *him.* Convincing herself he felt what she wanted him to feel, that he was acting on motivations as *she'd* act on them. How many millions of times had she done that, only to realize her mistake later?

Ask him, Laine. She'd had a revelation in Kevin's unlikely company. That this strange lack of real, intimate communication between them could be— was—partly her fault.

Ask him why he didn't want any women tonight. Find out for sure instead of guessing, instead of assigning him feelings she wanted him to have.

Her mouth opened; her throat muscles locked.

She was afraid. Afraid of what he'd say, either way. Afraid that if he didn't want any other woman but her, she'd be in danger again, more vulnerable than ever. On the other hand, afraid that he hadn't been with anyone else because the selection wasn't up to par and she'd come face to ugly face with not being as special to him as she wanted to be.

"You hungry? Want something to eat?"

She let out her breath, relieved and disappointed the moment was over. "No, thanks, I'm not hungry."

"Hang out and talk for a while?"

She should say no. Go into her room, close the door and read. Or focus on her date with Joe next week, or get herself to work up the nerve to sign on for skydiving. In her current mood, any intimate time with Grayson would put her at too much risk for when the inevitable seduction moves started. She might not be able to—or want to—fend him off.

Except that right now he didn't have a trace of the predatory look in his eyes. He seemed unusually serious. Almost uneasy. If he wasn't Grayson, she'd say he was feeling vulnerable himself. And her room would be safe, yes, but lonely, a place of brooding.

Brooding sucked.

"Okay." She made a gesture of surrender. "Just let me shower and change."

She showered off the sweat and tension of the evening, went into her bedroom refreshed and renewed, changed into the shorts and T-shirt she'd promised herself, and checked her e-mail, aware she was probably stalling.

From: Kathy Baker
Sent: Friday
To: Laine Blackwell; Angie Keller
Subject: This ex of yours

Well, I just KNOW what slut-puppy Angie's going to say about your ex. But I, the brilliant voice of reason, have to say do NOT sleep with him. I'm serious. You know what he's like, you've suffered through years of his crap, hello? Do we want to do that to ourselves again? No, we do not. This is your summer of fun, not your summer of being treated like garbage. Remember every mother out there says never marry a man expecting to change him. It doesn't happen. Mr. Tiger keeps his stripes. Mr. Leopard keeps his spots. Mr. Elephant never forgets his trunk...

Okay, I'm rambling. But you know I'm right! I'm hoping the Rich Guy worked out tonight. Let us know!

Later,
Kathy

From: Angie Keller
Sent: Friday
To: Laine Blackwell; Kathy Baker
Subject: re: This ex of yours

My, my, my. I just KNEW Miss-Priss Kathy was going to say stay away from the Grayster. BUT, if things didn't go well with your oh-so-Rich Guy tonight, think again. You and this stud-muffin were amazing together. Sex is sex and he's available. What could be better? You're older, wiser, you're not going to fall for his same old puppy tricks again. This time you're in control, girlfriend. He's there, he's hot, he's hungry. You go!

Oh, and just for the record, I got some last night. David the Construction Worker. Ooo-eee. I am one happy camper this morning. Details to follow.

God bless,
Angie

Laine grinned and pushed her computer chair back from the screen. They'd get details all right. Probably too many.

As for taking their advice, she felt like a cartoon character with an angel on one shoulder, a devil on the other. Kathy was right, Grayson probably couldn't change. But Angie was right, too. Laine was stronger now, and if nothing else, her Men To Do dates and all the single time in the past five years had shown her the kind of chemistry she had with Grayson didn't show up every day. Or year. Or decade.

Who knew? And why the hell was she sitting here doing all that brooding she hated? Why didn't she go practice what she'd been preaching to herself? Try to open lines of communication she had a hand in keeping shut. See if Grayson could listen. See if he could understand what she felt and what she feared. Any decision about what could happen between them would have to wait for that.

She stood, walked down the hallway and into the living room. He was worth giving this a try.

"Hi." She smiled at the sight of him, relaxed on the couch, two open beers, a bag of her favorite cheese-flavored popcorn, and his bare feet—all arranged neatly on her coffee table. This was more like the guy she once loved, less like the Bird of Prey he'd been for too long. "Looks like you managed to get the caps twisted off this time."

He eyed her strangely. "Twisted off?"

"I bought twist-off bottles after you had such a fit."

He shook his head, chuckling, and pointed to her

bottle opener near the popcorn. "And I was so proud I remembered."

Laine laughed, probably harder than the situation warranted, and flopped down beside him on the couch. It felt new and strange, old and familiar all at once, lounging next to him like this. She picked up her beer and took a sip she didn't really want. How the hell was she supposed to jump-start the topics she needed discussed?

Glad the weather cleared. Say, I was wondering, would you care to attempt some soul-bearing intimacy? And by the way, do you just want my tits and ass or is a real relationship okay?

"Where did you go to dinner tonight?"

"Wild Ginger." She propped her feet on the coffee table, a careful several inches from his.

"Didn't we go there once?"

"Ye-e-s." She started blushing at the memory she'd had to suppress in the restaurant tonight.

"Wasn't that the one with all the bamboo and the waterfalls?"

"Ye-e-s." *Where you tried to make me come under the table, and the waiter came over and asked if I was okay or if he should call a doctor.*

She waited. He'd bring it up.

"I liked that place." He finished a sip of beer and winked at her.

She braced herself for the lewd comment.

"So what's up with journalism school this fall? Are you excited?"

"Uh, yeah." She nodded, taken aback by his lack of lewdness. "It's going to be great."

"You don't sound very excited."

"Oh, well, I am."

His brows dropped down. "What gives, Laine? I know when you're excited. This is not excitement."

She shrugged. No way was she going to tell him that—

Wait. Stop. Wasn't this what she promised herself she wasn't going to do? Put bars across windows of intimacy?

"I...am excited. I think I would make a good reporter. I love to write, I love snooping, I love talking to people, and I'm not scared of being pushy when I need to be." She swept the air with her hand and let it fall. "It's just..."

"Yes?"

Laine sighed. This emoting stuff was hard. Why were they like this with each other? Why didn't it feel safe since they knew each other so well? Though, to be honest, she hadn't admitted a lot of these feelings even to herself before this.

She pulled her feet determinedly down from the table, turned her body to face him and took a preparatory breath. "It's just that this will be my third graduate program. I thought I wanted to go to medical school. I didn't last half a semester. I thought I wanted to write fiction. That time it took a year to convince me I didn't. So now...facing this..."

"You're afraid you won't like it."

"Yes." She cleared her throat. Crossed her legs. Uncrossed them. "I'm afraid I'm making another mistake trying to pin down my future before I know it really suits me."

"It's better than staying in a job you don't care about because you're scared to try."

"That's true." She pulled down the hem of her shorts, not meeting his eyes, feeling awkward and strange having this kind of conversation with him instead of their usual teasing chatter. "What about your job? You love that?"

"Oh, yeah." He put one hand behind his head and leaned it back. "I love what I do. I'm in charge, I lead the hunt, reel them in, convince them they want things they didn't know they wanted, then finish them off and on to the next. It's a great life."

Laine put her beer down, feeling a little sick. That pretty much summed up why she wasn't anxious to get involved with him again.

"I just need one huge company, one simpatico CEO of some mega-firm with ongoing needs for our services. I thought Omega Source would be it, but I think we're bombing there."

"Oh!" She slapped her thigh, relieved to be able to change the subject. "Speaking of CEOs, did I tell you I want to make dinner plans for you and me and Ben and Judy."

"Why is that 'speaking of CEOs'?"

"Ben. He's the CEO of Browning Systems."

Grayson put down his feet. "Bouquet Ben is Benton Carmichael, CEO of Browning Systems?"

"Yes."

He made a mask over his face with spread fingers. "Jeezus, Laine, why didn't you tell me? I've been trying to get in there for months now."

She rolled her eyes. "Well, gee, I don't know, maybe because I had no idea you were hunting him to add to your collection."

He put down his hands, held her gaze, his own speculative and slightly puzzled. "Sorry. I'd love to meet him. When were you thinking?"

"Next Thursday or Friday."

"I'm pretty sure I'll be in the city Thursday."

"Good. I want to fix him up with Judy, so don't spend the entire time trying to sell him."

"I promise." He held up three Scout's-honor fingers. "Though what makes you think he'll be able even to glance at Judy if he's after you?"

"He is *not* after me." She laughed at his teasing expression, her body relaxing into relief. This was so much easier to deal with.

"Oh, come on, look at those things." He indicated the latest magnificent bouquet. "Why on earth would he keep sending them if he wasn't into you?"

"We've been o-ver this." She sang the words in singsong impatience. "Because he knows I li-i-ike them. Because he knows they make me ha-a-ppy."

"Be serious."

"Why is it so hard for you to understand someone doing something nice for someone else?"

"I know how men are."

"Hello? News flash. Not all men are like you."

"You mean, predatory. Not interested in what comes after they make their catch."

"Exactly."

"Okay." He nodded, put his beer down and faced her, his dark eyes direct and serious. "You asked me two questions which I didn't answer the way I should have. One was, 'Is this all about the chase?' Remember?"

She threaded her fingers together and stared down at them. What was this, could he read her mind after all? "Yes."

"The answer is no. With you it was never about the chase." He held up his hands. "Okay, maybe on our very first dates in college. After that, there was messed-up shit at times, I admit, but you weren't ever just a chase for me, Laine.''

''Okay…'' Her heart started speeding up, but she couldn't tell if it was from excitement or fear. It felt like both. She unlaced her fingers and folded her arms.

''Second question—'And then what?' You wanted to know what would happen after we had sex.''

''Yes,'' she whispered. There was a weird buzzing in her head, a strange sense of disorientation, here in familiar surroundings. Something wasn't right. This wasn't the Grayson she knew.

''Here's what will happen—we'll have sex again. And again. And again. We'll hang out together. We'll do things, we'll go out to eat, we'll work out together. We won't have sex with other people because it's so damn good between us. When things get bad, we'll fight and work it out, get through it and go on, like normal couples do. That's what.''

She stared at his grave, handsome face, her eyes wide, body tight. He'd said everything she thought she wanted him to say, but their past still sat on her like a huge, immovable weight. How many times had he wanted to get back together and then been the one to back away? Though he'd never come out and committed himself like this, talked about the future, about staying together even in bad times. Usually he just seduced her and they were back on—until suddenly they weren't. But how could she trust him? How could she tell?

''Where did this come from?''

''I've been doing a lot of thinking.'' He gestured into the room, brought his hand back to his side. ''Figuring out what went wrong, what I did to make it that way, what's been going wrong again this time, why you were resisting me."

She rubbed her forehead, let it rest there on her fingertips. This was so strange. She wasn't reacting at all the way she thought she would. He was offering everything that had been holding her back and she was still afraid of moving forward.

"Here's another one. You want to know why I cheated on you in college?"

She swallowed, took in a sharp breath. "I thought you said you didn't know why."

He sighed. "I'm trying to give you what you want here, Laine. I told you, I've done a lot of thinking."

"Okay. I'm sorry. Go ahead."

"I cheated on you because I was twenty-two. I wasn't ready for a lifelong commitment. You practically had our china picked out."

She closed her eyes, made her mind go back. Had she been like that? She'd told him she loved him, mentioned a wedding… Yes. Guilty. But that's how she thought it was supposed to go.

"I…that's who I was then." She held her hands out in a shrug. "I thought life was like my mom and my sister said. Love equaled weddings, the sooner the better. I'm sorry."

"You don't have to be sorry." His voice turned tender, and she had to fight an absurd rush of tears. "What I did was inexcusable. But when you started talking marriage, I freaked. Went out and got myself drunk, Joanne attacked me, I didn't resist, you walked in…you know the rest."

She nodded. She understood. But understanding didn't bring her relief or closure. Instead the conversation had totally unnerved her. When she took away

Grayson the Manipulator, Grayson the Cheater, Grayson the Wrongdoer, what did she get?

No reason to stay away.

"So is this all okay now, Laine?"

"Yes."

"You clear on everything? Everything okay?"

She nodded, stared at her hands twisting in her lap.

"You don't look okay."

She pulled her head up, laughed at his quizzical expression. "I'm okay, I'm okay."

"Good." He clapped once and rubbed his hands together. "So we can have sex now?"

Her eyes went wide, instant outrage going full blast. "You…"

He shot his hand around the back of her neck, pulled her forward until their foreheads were touching. "I'm joking, Laine, relax."

"You…you…" She sputtered and grumbled, heard him chuckling and sputtered some more, feeling an answering smile fighting its way to her lips.

"Pig? Jerk? Manipulator?" His voice was low, his hand still circled her neck, holding her close.

"For a start." She didn't resist. It *was* okay now. Right? She could let herself start to trust him again. He hadn't gotten her back the way he always had in the past, with sexual manipulation. He'd been honest, made it clear they were both after the same thing— an exclusive ongoing relationship. So this was good. Very good.

He moved his chin forward, bringing his mouth closer. Stopped an inch away.

Laine closed her eyes, still sensing his nearness so vividly it was as if she could still see him. He'd done his part. She had to take this chance. There was no reason not to anymore.

She moved the rest of the way and met his lips. A light touch that burned a sexual thrill all the way down her body and swept away the remaining fear and hesitation. She wanted this, wanted him, more than she'd ever wanted anybody. That hadn't ever changed.

He increased the pressure between their lips, curled his arm around her neck, pressed her back against the couch, cradling her head in the crook of his elbow and kissing her like a starving man at the feast of his dreams.

She moaned, wrapped her arms around him and lost herself in the meeting of their mouths and tongues and bodies. How many times had she dreamed about this? Relived it? The passion between them was just as incredible as she remembered, maybe more for the delay while she resisted.

She twisted to the side, opened her legs, rocked against his long, hard thigh and knew there was no way she was going to tell him to stop tonight.

"Not here." He rolled her away and stood, extended his hand, eyes burning into hers. "Your bedroom."

"Yes." She let him pull her up, followed him down the hall to the door of his room, eager and reluctant, like a kid awaiting her first roller-coaster ride.

"You go on. I have to get condoms." He pulled her to him and kissed her, as if he couldn't bear even the tiniest separation.

"Okay. Yes." She watched him turn away, then rushed into her room, kicked out of her shorts and panties, yanked her T-shirt over her head, unhooked her bra and let it fall. Stretched as tall as she got, arms high, feeling her muscles expand, her lungs expand, her heart expanding. This would be okay. It would be okay.

She pulled her arms down, sat demurely on the bed, pulse pounding, legs crossed, hands covering her breasts, eyes cast down. Then, in a teasing and provocative way, lifted them when he came into the room. *You want me, here I am, come get me.*

He stopped in the doorway, wearing only shorts and a slow, sexy grin. "Oh my God, Laine, you have no idea how much I've wanted this."

She nodded, feeling an absurd swelling of teary happiness. "Yes, I do."

"Because you wanted it, too, or because you know what a dog I am?"

"Because I wanted it, too."

He moved across the room, knelt in front of her, looked up with a tender smile. "Hi."

"Hi." The word barely got past the emotion in her throat.

His smile faded; he leaned forward, dropped a slow kiss onto one bare knee, then the other, replaced each kissed spot with a hand. Then slid those large, warm hands slowly up her thighs, one all the way to her hip, the other until it encountered the impasse of her crossed legs.

"You remember that time we were in Wild Ginger?" His voice had dropped to the low, smooth tone he used to turn her on.

"Yes." God, it was working already.

He moved his hand farther, inched it in between her tightly closed thighs. "I wanted to make you come in the restaurant. Just from me touching you."

He pushed again so the tips of his fingers were nearly touching her sex. She gripped her muscles tighter, closed her eyes, kept her hands still over her breasts. "You didn't want me to, you were embarrassed, you kept your legs together like this, do you remember?"

"Yes."

He pushed farther. His fingers just brushed the lips of her sex. She resisted the urge to open, teasing herself, teasing him, making them both wait.

"I had to overcome your resistance then, too. By the time I found you, you were so wet, so hot."

She took long, shaky breaths, clamped her legs, felt his fingers thrust deeper, parting her, moving slightly against the pressure she exerted.

"Are you wet now?"

She nodded.

"Say it."

"I'm wet," she whispered. "You make me so wet."

He slid his free hand to the back of her waist, moved his other hand farther in. She whimpered, gave in, loosened her legs to give him better access.

"Oh, yes." He closed his eyes, let his fingers explore her gently, probing. "Let me in."

She let her head fall back, eyes closed. A sudden hard nip on the back of her hand made her yell and move it away. He swooped forward, captured her exposed breast in his mouth, sucked her nipple vigorously. The way he knew she loved it.

"Oh!" She opened her legs wide now, straining for him, turned on out of her mind. This man, this man...

He pressed her back on the bed, followed, rid himself of his shorts, moved to her other nipple, sucked and bit gently, then gradually with more pressure until she gave a grunt of pleasure-pain.

He lifted his head, looked into her eyes. Put his hands to her shoulders and dragged those hands over her breasts, her stomach, split them around her sex, rejoined them on her thighs in a slow journey to her feet. A long, hard, possessive stroke that said her body belonged to him.

She felt the fear rising again. Fear she'd disappear into him, fear he'd leave again.

She fought it, made herself open her legs wide, her sign she was ready. He gazed down at her exposed sex, trailed one finger over her curling hair, down her center. Then grabbed her knees, moved his arms under them, so her legs bent over his shoulders and his face was an inch from heaven.

"Tell me what you want."

"You know."

"Say it anyway."

"I want you to lick me till I come."

He grinned in triumph, lowered his head and moved his tongue in a lazy, lingering path, starting at her clitoris, parting her lips, moving over her sex, lifting her hips and finishing down over her other sensitive opening.

She moaned and offered herself again.

He let his tongue play, worked her top to bottom, her clit, her sex, the sensitive skin below her female opening, then lower where no other man had been, stopping when she got too close to her climax, teasing, tasting, stopping again, until she was a panting, writhing mess.

"Grayson." She nearly shouted his name, clutched the bedspread in her fists.

"What is it?"

"Let me come."

"No."

"Why?"

"This is your punishment for going after other men when you belong to me."

"Bastard."

"That's Mr. Bastard to you."

She laughed helplessly, loving his play dominance. In a flash she realized that sex with them was always about control. About power. They got together for sexual combat, rarely made love or shared themselves. Right now it was a blessing—all she could handle.

"Make me come or I do it myself." She moved her hand to her clit, started to rub eagerly.

"In your dreams." He grabbed her fingers away, moved up so he was kneeling astride of her chest, and pinned her arms to her sides with his folded legs. "Not until I get some fun."

"No way." She moved her head, trying not to give herself away by laughing. "Me first."

He smiled the smile of the devil to the damned. "Open wide."

"Say please."

He chuckled and moved so his erection stroked her cheek. She felt its weight, its heat, and knew she'd give in to the chance to pleasure him.

"Please, Laine."

"Yes, sir, Mr. Bastard." She turned her head to where his penis lay along her cheek and took it inside her mouth. He moaned, closed his eyes, loosened his legs' grip on her arms.

She pulled them free and used one hand to help

stroke him, the other to cup his balls, fondle them, stretch and stroke the skin down from the base of his penis, manipulate the small tender sacs inside. She had the power now. She was in charge.

He moaned again, thrust gently with his hips. His look of bliss became pained. Perspiration made a sheen on his face.

She pulled back and grinned. He had more staying power than any man she'd been with, probably even more now that he was older, but by the look of it, she was severely testing his control.

"What's the matter, can't last anymore?"

"Not this time." He moved back, grabbed the condom off her windowsill, tore it open, pulled it on and lunged to lie over her, poised to enter. Then stopped. Looked down into her eyes.

Tenderness, affection and vulnerability. "Laine."

Something piercing and sweet barely registered before adrenaline shot through her. And panic.

"No. Not like this." She wriggled out from under him. Got on her hands and knees, body trembling. "I want it this way. Hard. You know how I like it."

He stayed next to her on the bed, his breathing rough, uneven. From across the room her computer chimed the arrival of an e-mail. A car horn blared outside, followed by the shouted curses of a pedestrian. "Not this time, Laine."

"Do it." She wiggled her ass invitingly, looked at him with pleading eyes. "I want it this way."

Another long moment where he stared at her in that strange new way, as if he was reading her mind.

"Please, Grayson."

He sat up, got on his knees and her breath came out in a rush. She was safe.

"Okay. *This* time you can have it your way."

He positioned himself behind her, gripped her hips and guided her onto him. He thrust and she cried out with pleasure. She couldn't handle sweet face-to-face missionary right now. Not with him. Not this soon, with their reunion so new and untested.

She put her elbows down, braced herself on the bed, to take the force of his pounding.

"Oh." It was perfect. Her body jerked forward with each thrust, her breasts swung, his skin slapped hers. *"Yes."*

He kept up the fierce rhythm, while she was able to push her feelings and fears away, lose herself in sexual sensation.

She reached her hand back, cupped his balls to push him over the edge. He groaned and reached for her shoulders, pulled her up back against him, found her clitoris and started rubbing.

"Oh." Perspiration broke out on her body. "Oh!"

She was gone. The orgasm built slowly, stretched long and hot and endless before she cried out again and contracted around him.

He slowed the rubbing, sensing the pace of her comedown, then stopped, pushed her limp body onto the bed, collapsed behind her on his side, his big muscular arms around her, trapping her tenderly.

"Sweetheart." He whispered the word into her hair, found his way inside her again, slowly this time, thrust gently for one long, lovely minute, then faster for one more, before he tensed into his own climax, cradling her all the while.

She lay, drenched, in the circle of his arms for a

sated, blissful moment before it occurred to her that in all the years she'd known him, he'd never called her sweetheart.

And the fear kicked in all over again.

9

MA VOITURE est comfortable et rapide.

Laine rolled her eyes at her French workbook spread in front of her on her bed. Yes, her car was comfortable and fast. So what was *le point?*

Où est Jean? Là bas, dans la voiture noire. C'est ça voiture? Mais non, la voiture de Jean est bleue.

Where is that bastard, John? Late again? Is that *his* black car there? *Mon Dieu*, it's a pimpmobile, John has become *très* naughty! But no, the car of John is blue. Therefore we may maintain a G-rating with this material.

Ugh.

Laine flung the workbook on her desk and rolled over onto her back to stare at the ceiling. She'd cancelled her usual Saturday lunch with Judy today. After two nights with Grayson and waking up next to him this morning only hours ago, she couldn't picture herself trying either to hide or explain to Judy what was going on. She wasn't even sure herself.

The sex was amazing, incredible, inventive and erotic. That hadn't changed. But he had, or she had, or they had. Something was different. They weren't as easy-breezy together, not as natural. There was an edgy intensity about their sex and a nervousness in their conversation that hadn't ever been there before.

Were they going to ruin everything all over again by having crossed the line?

Who knew? All she did know was that she couldn't tolerate the kind of analysis Judy would immediately take it upon herself to perform. Judy would read all kinds of things into their reunion. Grill Laine on her feelings and her expectations for the future, blahblah-blah. She'd always wanted Laine and Grayson to work out permanently. Within minutes of hearing they'd spent one weekend back in the sack together, she'd be planning Laine's bachelorette party. What was it with women and their wedding lust? Just like Mom and Laine's sister, Mimi. They wanted other people to validate their dull lives by joining in the non-fun.

Laine turned onto her stomach and propped her head on her hands, knees bent, heels waving aimlessly. If she had her way, Judy and Ben would fall instantly in love on Thursday to give Judy something else to think about. Like her own bachelorette party.

Right now Laine just wanted to spend some Zen time. Enjoy being back together with Grayson and try to deal with the uncertainty the best way she could. Even if it seemed sometimes the best way to deal with that uncertainty was to ignore it.

She hauled herself off the bed and sat listlessly at her computer. Sooner or later she'd have to tell the Men To Do girls what had happened with Grayson, though they'd seen it coming a long way away. Probably longer than she had. Maybe they'd be able to respond in a less here-comes-the-bride way than Judy.

She opened her e-mail program and typed.

From: Laine Blackwell
Sent: Saturday
To: Angie Keller; Kathy Baker
Subject: Sex with the Ex

Well, things with Grayson have heated up sort of abruptly. Well, okay, not that abruptly. The tension has been building for a while, but I wasn't really coming clean with you guys on how tempted I was. I really wanted to find a Man To Do and be part of the gang. It fit the summer I planned so perfectly. But then he—

Laine took her fingers off the keyboard. He what? She what? How could she go into all this?

He was honest about things he'd never been honest about before, and so I—

No. That would make no sense. Sounded utterly stupid to boot.

I felt I should give him a chance because—

Laine deleted the e-mail and closed the program. Forget it. She'd have to explain all the thought processes, how he'd changed, how she felt, how she thought things might be different, how she didn't want them to be too different, and on and on. There was no way for any of it to be remotely comprehensible, especially when she wasn't even sure she understood it herself.

Then she'd have to deal with the girls' responses. Either overcome their objections and defend her decision to risk giving in to her attraction, or sit back and watch them run with the concept, probably further than would make her comfortable just yet.

She stood quietly, left her room, kicking aside the tap shoes she'd put in her path to remind herself to practice, and went into the kitchen. Her apartment felt stuffy and confining, even with the windows open. But she didn't feel like going out. Except she didn't feel like staying in, either. Her yoga routine would be a good idea, but even the road to inner peace didn't appeal.

Grayson had invited her to spend the rest of the weekend with him in Princeton, but she'd refused. She needed this alone time to figure out what was going on. Regain her balance before she got so sucked into his powerful allure that she lost herself, the way she'd lost herself to him so many times before. Already the signs were showing. She couldn't concentrate, she wasn't that interested in her work, her classes. Two nights of sex and she was ready to turn into the lifeless man-serving drudges her mother and sister had become.

Oh, look how strong and independent she'd turned out to be.

Not.

Except she *was,* that was the problem—as long as there wasn't a penis in her life.

She opened the refrigerator door. Something for lunch… Something…

No Clark's Diner chicken soup in the house; she'd blown the chance to have that comfort when she'd cancelled with Judy. She had leftover braised pork chops with apricots and sour cream from her cooking class experiment. Grayson had said he enjoyed it, even though the sauce curdled when she let it boil by mistake. She could heat that up.

Laine sighed. Nah. Tuna sandwich. She got out the sandwich fixings and moved the wobbly, unevenly-glazed pottery bowl she'd made in her class to the side of her counter so she'd have more room. Potting had not turned out to be her strong point. Or French. Or cooking. Or tap dancing. Nor was she keeping up with the yoga, even when she needed it. As far as skydiving, why not just admit that she'd probably wet herself or throw up all over the instructor if she tried to jump out of a plane?

Okay. Honesty time. This summer of fun wasn't quite what she expected. Grayson wasn't what she expected. Worse, she missed him, and he'd left only an hour or so ago.

What was it about getting involved with someone that turned her into a sniveling, weak-kneed, pathetic doormat?

She grimaced and scraped the can of tuna into a non-wobbly metal bowl. Slopped some mayonnaise over it.

This feeling of being incomplete was horrible. She totally resented that she wasn't perfectly happy doing what she wanted to be doing, namely living life to its fullest and exploring her potential. She'd even had a twinge of regret canceling the Men To Do date with Joe the Silent Stud for next week. Though Antonio and Kevin had looked like a lot of fun, too, and they had turned out not to be, so who knew. She might as well face that she and Grayson had something pretty extraordinary, and until they'd worked through it one way or another, other men would suffer in comparison.

She mixed the mayonnaise and tuna together, and readied two pieces of bread. Her greatest fear right now was that they'd never work it through. That they'd spend their lives attaching and detaching, never achieving total intimacy or total separation.

God, what a depressing thought. Laine scooped canned fish and mayonnaise onto the bread, not even in the mood to chop onion and celery and pickle, her usual must-haves in a tuna sandwich.

She needed to make sure she and Grayson did things differently this time. She wasn't going to spend every night with him. Wasn't going to turn the rest of her life off to please him, okay, not that he ever asked her to—which was the most pathetic part of it.

They'd go forward, sure, yes, great, but as friends who happened to be lovers, not Siamese twins. She'd keep going at full-tilt, the way she always did, and find a way to fit him into the cracks of free time she had, not design him as the centerpiece of her existence. If potting and French and cooking and tap dancing and screwing random males weren't her things, she could shop around for other ways to spend time. She was a woman of many talents. A Renaissance chick. Something would take.

She couldn't forget the kind of man Grayson was, the kind of relationship they'd always had. Just because he'd opened up a little this time, and seemed to be making an effort to be more communicative, didn't mean he'd automatically become perfect for her.

Right?

She took the sandwich and a glass of milk into her living room, thinking that at some point she should change out of her pajamas and at some point she ought to work out. She turned on the TV, found the Katharine Hepburn/Spencer Tracy movie *Adam's Rib* and settled in to watch. Her wild, fun summer of a lifetime was going on as planned, a breathtaking delight every hour of every day.

Laine yawned and took a sip of her milk. Maybe starting this afternoon.

GRAYSON GOT OFF THE TRAIN at Penn Station and joined the throng making its way along the dark, dingy platform to the escalator. Dinner tonight at Nougatine Restaurant with Laine, Judy and Ben. If he played it right, if Ben was receptive and Browning Systems had any need for Jameson's services, this night could be huge. He'd promised Laine not to interfere with her matchmaking efforts and he'd honor that promise. But it seemed to him no harm could come from a little exploration into the topic. At the very least he could ask to drop by and see Ben, maybe talk to his marketing people. An "in" like this was too important to waste.

The only possible glitch would be if Grayson's instincts were correct and Ben was going along with the blind date idea tonight just to get closer to Laine. In that case, Grayson might as well shoot himself down now and get it over with.

He stepped off the escalator and strode through Penn Station, dodging people, enjoying the adrenaline the city always produced in him. Thrilling place, though he couldn't live here 24/7 anymore. His peace and slice of green in Princeton fit him better now. He was glad Laine agreed to come back with him after the meal tonight—a chance to take in how it felt having her in his home. He'd been thinking about asking her to move in with him. The idea appealed more and more, after he pushed past the initial frat-boy resistance and asked himself deep down what he wanted.

To his surprise the answer had surfaced fairly quickly. Maybe Ted—the ultimate player, who'd chosen to settle down and seemed so happy—had a hand in breaking through Grayson's resistance to happily ever after. Maybe it was just seeing Laine again. Making love to her and remembering how good it was between them, how well they knew each other.

Except something was seriously bugging her. Their lovemaking had been fiery, exciting—it always was— but every time he'd tried to make it about Laine and Grayson, instead of about bodies and orgasms, she'd balked. He wanted to understand that, he wanted to help her through it. If it was something he was doing, he wanted to change it.

And if that didn't make him madly, deeply and maturely in love, he didn't know what did. No point pretending this was about anything else. He loved Laine, he always had. They'd never managed to get each other at the right time in the right frame of mind, but while he'd always accepted that before—hell, he'd been most of the problem—this time he was determined they'd make it work.

He emerged from the crowds in Penn Station to the crowds on Eighth Avenue and headed north. The evening was warm but dry and unusually clear, with a soft wind blowing. He'd much rather walk than take the subway. And he was early anyway.

Twenty-four blocks later and right on time, he went up the steps and into the glass-and-steel Trump Tower. A short, pudgy, middle-aged balding guy waited in the building's entranceway, near the hostess podium outside the restaurant. Short, pudgy, middle-aged and balding, but with a suit that fit his round body to perfection and an air of confidence that fit him even better.

"Benton Carmichael?" Grayson extended his hand in greeting.

"Call me Ben." The deep voice boomed out; Ben smiled and pumped Grayson's hand, eye contact direct and open. No suspicion, no jealousy. Good sign. "Glad to meet you. Heard a lot about you."

"From Laine?" Call him territorial, but Grayson couldn't quite get enthusiastic about the idea of Laine discussing him with He Who Sends Flowers.

"No, no. From Judy."

Grayson raised his brows. "You've met her?"

"I called her when Laine told me she wanted to set us up. I thought she'd be more at ease tonight if we had the chance to chat first."

"Nice of you."

Ben shrugged and cleared his throat into his fist. "Just want her to be comfortable. Blind dates can be hard on the nerves."

"Absolutely." Grayson let the impression linger that this was how he operated, too, aware he never would have thought of calling first if the blind date was his. Though he used the same technique in sales as a matter of course. Do your homework, know your prospects before the first meeting. Forethought, strategy, then action. Obviously, Ben thought the same way, which was why the flowers he sent Laine still made Grayson suspicious.

"So, Grayson, Laine tells me you're in sales. Multimedia."

Grayson nodded. *Here we go.* "And Laine tells me you're CEO of Browning Systems."

"Yessir. Been there five years now."

"And you've done good things for them...so far."

A slow smile spread over Ben's soft face. "You think you can help us do better."

"Yes, I do." He returned the smile calmly. Most people thought sales professionals incapable of anything but relentless brute force. He liked to prove them wrong. "My partner, Chuck Gartner, and I started Jameson Productions six months ago. We're already on target to do a half-million in business this year."

"Impressive. I've been thinking for a while that our marketing plan and Web site in particular could use an overhaul. I'll tell you what I'm anxious about, though, Grayson." Ben regarded him from under his bushy brows like a teacher about to deliver a lecture of great importance. "This particular Web site is very special to me. And it hasn't been treated well by companies like yours in the past."

Grayson tried not to look incredulous. Treated well? Was this a Web site or an abuse victim? "I see."

"This...*Web site,*" Ben emphasized the words, "needs someone who won't just fix her up and leave again. She needs someone who is going to make a commitment, be there for the long haul, when she's up and running, sure, but also when she crashes. Even if you have your hands full of other things at the time. Am I making myself clear?"

Grayson suppressed a chuckle. Ben was talking about Laine. Talking about her like a concerned father, not a competitor. So what *was* up with the damn flowers? "Perfectly clear. Jameson Productions is interested in a committed, mutually rewarding relationship."

"Good." Ben's stern expression lightened. "So long as we understand each other on that."

"We do."

"Excellent. Come by and see me. Make an appointment. I'll collar our people to hear what you have to say."

"I'll give you a call on Monday." Grayson wore a pleasant smile while his insides were doing a sideline cheer. He was in! Only about a thousand percent more easily than he feared. All he'd had to do was to promise to love, honor and cherish both the Web site and Laine. Nothing more or less than what he'd been planning anyway.

"Ah, here we are." Ben looked past Grayson, and his face brightened.

Grayson swung around and experienced that same rush of emotion he always did when he saw Laine. She looked incredible. Fresh and sweet and dynamite sexy in a flowery minidress that clung to her body as she moved. Judy looked as he remembered, shy and pretty with a voluptuous figure and a terrific smile. He greeted her with a warm hug and the expected catch-up questions, waited while Laine supervised official introductions between Judy and Ben, then slipped his arm around Laine's waist, tugged her to him and kissed her temple. "Hi."

"Hi." She tipped her head back and met his eyes. He made no effort to hide what he was feeling. Just let it shine on, like the harvest moon. For maybe three seconds she returned his gaze, then her expression grew wary, she blinked, looked away and moved out of his embrace to announce their arrival to the hostess.

What was that? Why was she being so damn skittish? Did she still doubt he was serious about her? Even with his track record he thought he'd made it clear this time was different. Maybe she felt awkward being affectionate in front of Judy and Ben, who were meeting for the first time. Though they seemed to be chatting away like old friends absorbed in a reunion.

The hostess seated them at a table near the tan-wood-and-glass bar, Grayson next to Laine and across from Judy. The waiter arrived and offered menus.

"Here it comes." Ben beamed at Judy, who giggled and blushed.

"Here what comes?"

"That weird silence after you get your menus," Judy answered Laine, gazing at Ben as if they were already lovers. "We were talking about how awkward it is—"

"—when you want to be talking, but at the same time you're trying to read your menu—"

"—and you can't tell what's worse, silence or ordering something you haven't had time to choose carefully."

"Hmm." Laine tipped her head to look at Grayson. "You and I never really had to deal with that on our first date."

"Nope." He winked at her. Their first date had been a late-night, pizza-and-beer feast with roommates in attendance, followed by three hours of sex— without roommates in attendance.

Those were the days. Now if he ate three-quarters of a pizza and drank a pitcher, he'd be up all night because of indigestion, not sex.

The waiter reappeared, searching for drink orders.

Ben gestured gallantly to Judy. "The lady will have a glass of Domaine La Perriere Sancerre 2000. Am I right?"

"I had my eye on that one, yes." Judy glowed with pleasure. "And for the gentleman…a glass of the Paringa 2001 Shiraz?"

"Perfect."

The waiter wrote down the orders and looked expectantly between Laine and Grayson, obviously not sure who would order for whom.

"What will I have, Grayson?" Laine grinned, but he couldn't help feeling this was some kind of test. How the hell was he supposed to know what she was in the mood for?

"Ah. Well. The lady next to me will have a glass of your 2004 vintage, brewery-bottled Budweiser."

Laine rolled her eyes. "Champagne, please. And for the wise-guy, a Tanqueray martini, very dry, straight up with a twist."

He grinned, not wanting to show his discomfort. The beer was a joke, but she did drink champagne at nicer places; he should have remembered that. She had him pegged with the martini, no question.

"So, Ben and Judy." Laine settled her elbows on the table and rested her head on clasped fingers. "It seems like you got to know each other fast."

"We did hit it off pretty quickly." Ben smiled at Judy while he spoke. "But I wouldn't say we know each other yet. That takes time."

"Do you think you can ever know someone completely?" Judy asked. "Even after years and years?"

Grayson put his foot out until it nudged Laine's. What hadn't they done together? Been through together? They'd known each other all their adult lives. Even the five years apart hadn't changed things between them much.

Laine's foot didn't nudge him back. "It's pretty rare."

He started to smile, but her expression caught him. It wasn't quite the smug but-*we've*-achieved-it look he expected. Did she mean they *didn't* know each other?

"But do you think it's possible?" Judy toyed with her empty wineglass, glancing coyly at Ben. "To be intimate on every level?"

Laine shrugged. "I'm not really sure."

Grayson removed his foot from alongside hers. What the hell was she talking about? What did they have if not total intimacy? Okay, maybe they needed a readjustment ping or two, but if anything, they were closer than they'd ever been since they'd agreed to go forward together.

"It's absolutely possible." Ben spoke with CEO authority. "Two people can know each other inside out. In fact, for a really successful relationship, it should be a given."

The two women gazed at Ben as if he were the next Messiah. Once again, this time without even opening his mouth, Grayson had failed some test he didn't know he was taking. Already this was starting to be a very long evening.

The waiter brought their drinks, in the nick of time as far as Grayson was concerned, and the "intimacy" discussion was abandoned in favor of toasts to future friendships—with meaningful glances between Ben and Judy—and the pleasure of first sips.

"I still haven't thanked you enough for all the

flowers, Ben.'' Laine put her champagne flute down carefully. "They cheered the place up so much. Especially when spring was taking forever and everybody hated everybody else.''

Ben threw back his head and laughed richly. The guy would make a perfect Santa Claus at Christmas.

"I'm glad they made you happy. I'm sure Grayson will enjoy taking that over.''

Laine smiled into the sudden silence. Grayson ground his teeth together. Sorry. He wasn't going to be railroaded into taking over another man's gesture.

"Well, in any case,'' Ben hurried on, "someday you'll be able to make your wish come true yourself.''

"What wish is that?'' Grayson tried very hard to keep from sounding like the nerd left out of the big joke.

Ben laughed again. *Ho-ho-ho.* "I'm sure I don't have to tell you.''

Laine shot Grayson an impatient look. Okay, so sue him. Obviously he was supposed to know something he didn't.

"Ben, you remembered my wish?'' Laine put a hand to her chest. "Is that why you sent them? You are so sweet.''

He waved her off. "I just listened to what you wanted.''

"That's a pretty rare quality.'' Laine took another sip of her drink, not looking at Grayson.

He narrowed his eyes. Welcome to the Skewer Grayson Hour. Except, as usual, he didn't know what he'd done. Somehow he was apparently supposed to know Laine wanted flowers without being told.

Damn it, he hated this. All these rules women made

up, then were angry you broke when you didn't even know what they were.

"Laine always says she wants to be just rich enough to take taxis whenever she feels like it, travel spontaneously and have fresh flowers in the house every week." Judy sounded embarrassed having to explain it to him. As if he were an ancient auntie who had forgotten how to tie her shoe.

"I never heard that." He looked over at Laine. "You never told me that."

"I didn't?"

"No, Laine. I would have remembered."

She dropped her eyes. Her turn to look abashed. But any thrill of victory didn't last long. Deep down he knew that even if she had told him during one of their times together, he would not have searched for a way to make her dream come true. He would have said, "Oh, yeah?" and tried to cop a feel. No wonder she was wary about moving too far too fast.

"So, Laine." Judy jumped into the awkward silence. "How are all your adventures going this summer?"

Laine pasted on a smile. "Great! Totally great. I love everything I'm doing. The yoga, pottery, cooking, French lessons…"

"No skydiving?" Judy gave an exaggerated shudder.

"Not yet."

"You're like a hummingbird." Ben gestured into the air toward Laine. "Beautiful and quick, flitting from one thing to another."

Laine laughed and lifted her champagne in a toast. "Here's to doing everything there is to do before we die."

"I don't know about doing everything." Judy didn't reach for her glass to join the toast. "I'd rather do less for longer."

Ben nodded. "Same here. I like to latch on to a few things, then run with them."

"Another thing we have in common." Judy did lift her glass then, to Ben. "I've never been one for playing the field."

"Me, neither." Ben clinked with her. "I've had one apartment since college, two jobs, and I've been waiting patiently for the right woman to come along. A lifelong commitment is the most important and potentially fulfilling aspect of one's life—I don't believe in wasting time with people who are wrong for me."

"I agree." Judy nodded vehemently, eyes glowing into Ben's smile. It was entirely possible spontaneous wedding vows were about to be exchanged.

"Interesting." Laine frowned and turned to Grayson. "How do you feel about that?"

Grayson drained his martini. This test he wasn't going to fail. Commitment, the ultimate human fulfillment? No one had ever put the subject to him like that before. He loved his career, he loved his hobbies, his friends, but was there anything in the world more important to him, or to his future, than Laine?

No.

"I agree with Ben and Judy." He took Laine's cold hand under the table and gave it a squeeze, anticipating her joy and relief. "Maybe it took me a while to come over to that point of view, but I definitely agree."

"You do?" Laine sounded shocked.

Was that good or bad?

"Yes." He leaned over and kissed her cheek. "I do."

She nodded somberly, eyes wide, face tense, not at all joyous. And the only relief that crossed her face was when the waiter came to ask for their orders and interrupted the moment.

All right. Enough. He couldn't get her alone soon enough, and for once not just to get his dick in her.

He, Grayson Alexander, actually wanted to have a talk.

The faster they got back to his house in Princeton, the better, so he could find out what she was thinking, what she was afraid of, and reassure her as best he could. Once again he thought he'd figured out what she wanted from him—a commitment to exploring their future together—and had been surprised and happy to find it was what he wanted, too.

Once again, she hadn't reacted as he'd expected.

They placed their orders for the chef's tasting menu, chatted more, then were treated to course after superb course. How he lasted through it, he hadn't a clue. Ben and Judy did most of the talking, continuing to agree on everything from food to philosophy, passions to politics. After dessert, Grayson played a friendly game of no-let-me-pay with Ben over the check, lost graciously and promised to call on Monday. Outside the restaurant, he hailed a cab and rode with Laine to Penn Station, on time to catch the 10:37 p.m. train to Princeton.

They dropped into seats just as the doors closed. Grayson leaned back and took Laine's hand, laced their fingers together and smiled over at her. She looked tired, solemn and unbelievably beautiful.

"Your matchmaking instinct was right on. From what I could see, Ben and Judy are practically engaged."

Laine chuckled, then sat in silence until a small sigh escaped her that sounded more wistful than satisfied. "She'll be treated like a queen."

"And what, I treat you like a royal concubine?"

"That's not what I meant."

She might have smiled to take away the barb, but he had a feeling deep down it was exactly what she meant. "Look, Laine. I'm just not a flowers-every-week kind of guy. It doesn't mean I don't care about you."

"I know." She looked out at the darkness of the tunnel under the city.

"You want to tell me what's bothering you?"

She shot him a surprised look, but whether it was because she didn't think he'd notice or because she didn't think he'd ask, he couldn't tell. Either way it was a moot point. He had noticed and he was asking. And this was the kind of man he wanted to be for her from now until death did them part.

"Nothing. I'm fine."

He gritted his teeth. "Laine, I know you. Something is—"

"I don't think you do, Grayson. Not really."

He let go of her hand. "What the hell does that mean?"

"Nothing. Never mind."

"Never mind? Are you kidding me? You say something like that and expect me to ignore it?"

"We've always been really good together. In bed. But the rest of it…" She shrugged.

He fought down a surge of anger. She couldn't dismiss everything between them with a shrug. There was still plenty holding them together besides sex. Yes, there were problems, but he felt more ready than ever to work through them. "Why do you think that is?"

"I don't know. We just can't seem to...open up to each other."

Grayson took a deep breath. There wasn't another human on the planet he felt closer to. What more did she want? "Okay, so maybe we shouldn't think of this as picking up where we left off. Maybe we need to pretend we're starting from the beginning."

She did a half nod, clearly unconvinced. "Maybe that's best."

"Okay." He took her hand again, this time she squeezed his back. Damn it, this would work. "Do we have to go all the way back to introductions?"

She laughed, though unwillingly. "No."

"First kiss?"

"Done that."

He pitched his voice to a low suggestive whisper. "Have we had sex?"

She turned slowly to meet his eyes, hers half closed and sultry. He knew that look. He was starting to get hard already.

"No sex yet."

"So I get to seduce you for the first time?"

Her nostrils flared. Her eyes darkened. "Yes."

"Mmm." A picture immediately came to mind. Going home, showing Laine his house. His living room, kitchen, dining room and finally his bedroom. Moving closer, kissing, touching. Taking off her clothes, one piece at a time, and lingering over the parts newly exposed. Making long, slow love to her in his own bed, showing her how he felt with his body, his mouth and his tongue. Making her understand that he was here for her, that she was safe with him no matter how long this took to get right.

"Now," she whispered. "Here."

He shot a startled glance around at the crowded train. "That's what you want?"

"Yes." Her eyes shone with excitement. Her hand crept up onto his thigh; her own parted slightly.

His dick reacted further, even as his mind hesitated. She drove him wild like no other woman he'd ever known. And the thought that they could share this kind of intimacy with no one around them the wiser got him off even more.

Except that today...

"Now, Grayson. I want it now."

Her whisper undid him. He took off his jacket, draped it over her lap like a blanket, pushed his hand under and slid the hem of her skirt slowly up her bare legs, following the firm, smooth line of her thighs.

He nearly passed out when he found she wasn't wearing panties.

"You planned this."

She sent him a naughty temptress's grin. He returned it halfheartedly. At any other time he would have been delighted. Taken it as another sign of how compatible they were, both up for matters sexual anyplace, anytime. But tonight it didn't feel right. It didn't jibe with the long, slow romantic seduction he wanted, wearing his heart out on his sleeve and only the two of them there to share it.

Laine's tongue crept out and made a long, slow journey around her lips. Her eyes pleaded; she shifted against his hand.

Okay. He could make love to her the way he wanted to, later at his house, and still please her now.

He settled himself back in the seat to look as natural as possible with his fingers doing the walking. An elderly woman lurched down the aisle, met his eyes and smiled at the same time his fingers found Laine. She was wet, warm, her legs opened at his touch. He glanced at her. Her head was tipped away from him, resting against the back of the seat, eyes closed.

He moved his finger in slow circles, felt her hips lift in response. His penis hardened further. He crossed his legs to hide the bulge, moved his finger down, pretending to change position, found her female opening and pushed in.

She gasped quietly, hunched down in the seat, arched against his finger. He pulled out after a few more thrusts, found her clit again and resumed the slow stroking.

A low moan left her throat. The train swayed around a turn; his finger worked. He glanced at her again, at her dark lashes fluttering on her cheek as she tried in vain to look relaxed and sleeping, at her heightening color, at her chest heaving as she got close.

He loved her, loved her sense of adventure, her energy, her carefully hidden vulnerability, everything about her. Later in bed together, skin to skin, he promised himself and her silently, it would all be very different.

The train accelerated. His fingers kept pace, moving harder and faster as he sensed her nearing the edge.

"Oh!" She kept the word quiet, but he knew it had cost her not to cry out.

He turned to watch her, thrust his finger again inside her, pushing hard in a sex-rhythm, then pulled out again to concentrate on her clitoris and send her over.

"Oh." Her eyes shot open wide, her mouth worked soundlessly, she stared out the train window, obviously not registering anything but the bliss of her own climax.

Nothing else. Not the trees, not the passing towns, not the other passengers.

Not even him.

10

Laine let her head loll against the headrest of Grayson's Honda, which they'd retrieved after getting off the train at Princeton Junction. She hadn't been in Princeton for several years, and an eerie sense of coming home mixed with the strange mood she'd been in all evening, like oil and water.

She couldn't quite place the cause of her mood, and couldn't say she liked herself this way. She hadn't meant to give Grayson a hard time in the restaurant. But something about Ben's gentle kindness and the way Judy responded to him—the way they responded to each other—put an angry pain in Laine's heart.

Envy was a damaging, useless emotion, she knew, but she couldn't help wishing she and Grayson could be more honest and open like that. She couldn't help being annoyed at him, even though it was pointless and childish. He wasn't able to become someone else any more than she was.

And yet the moment when he'd said he agreed that two people together was the most important thing in the world… The statement was so out of character, she hadn't even known how to react except with shock and uncertainty.

On the train home he'd been even more open, wanting her to talk about her feelings. And her response, faced with the Grayson she'd always wanted him to be, had been deep resistance, fear of letting him that far into her head. Was he for real? Or was he being Mr. Salesman, absorbing Ben's strategy and echoing it to his advantage? She didn't know, and the entire evening had unsettled and exhausted her. Not until she'd seduced him into the safe familiarity of sex had the world turned right side up again.

She closed her eyes briefly and made herself shake off the anxiety, tired of trying to figure everything out, wishing she could pitch the pain and betrayal of their last go-around once and for all and give herself over more easily to trusting him this time.

Eyes back open, determined to keep the brooding at bay, she peered out at the attractive storefronts lining Nassau Street, Princeton's main thoroughfare. To her New Yorker's eyes, it looked like a ghost town. Only a few pedestrians strolled the sidewalks. "Looks like Princeton is still not noted for its nightlife.

"I'm glad we're arriving late. Downtown has become a traffic nightmare in the last decade or so."

"Ugh." Laine wrinkled her nose at the thought of the sleepy college town transformed.

"You get used to it. It's still a wonderful place to live."

"I'm sure." As in "sure she'd go nuts." No noise, no excitement, no feeling of being in the center of it all. She loved stepping outside her building's front door bang into life-in-progress.

When she'd been seventeen, the peace and safety of the town and campus had been one of the reasons she'd chosen to attend Princeton. She'd changed a lot since seventeen, though she had to admit that the quiet, the lush trees and green expanses—black right now in the darkness—made her feel closer to peaceful and relaxed than she'd felt in...well, who knew?

She yawned and leaned her head against the glass to gaze up at the brilliant array of stars—thousands more than the bright lights of Manhattan allowed to compete in their sky.

"Tired?" Grayson turned off Nassau Street onto Snowden Lane.

"Mmm." The tender concern in his voice made her smile and relax even further. "The champagne did me in."

"We're almost there. I can't wait to show off the place. And it's supposed to be a beautiful day tomorrow. We can go kayaking on the canal."

"Sounds great." She'd have her energy back tomorrow. After a good night's sleep. Though she and Grayson had a way of finding things to do other than sleeping. Look what happened even to an innocent train ride.

"Here we are."

He pulled up to a two-story, split-level—in the darkness she couldn't tell if it was yellow or white— with shutters that looked black. A low stone wall bordered the driveway, tiny-leafed vines tumbling over it like little waterfalls.

She got out into the cool, fresh, green-smelling air and stretched, listening with delight to the chirping of crickets, grinning at the sight of fireflies flickering around the dim shapes of bushes across the street. It reminded her of arriving home in Cincinnati from a long family trip, hurling herself out of the stale car smell into the cool, suburban night air. Then she and her sister would race inside while her parents unpacked the car to discover that everything looked the same and yet different somehow than when they had left.

Except this wasn't her home, it belonged to Grayson.

"Come on in."

She dragged her overnight bag out of the back seat and followed Grayson up the flagstone walkway to the front door, inhaling the wonderful flowery smells of his front garden. Rhododendrons, it looked like, peonies, spruce shrubs and azaleas—all she could recognize in the dim light.

"This is beautiful." She gestured to the beds, showing green here and there in the light of strategically placed lanterns. "The people you bought the place from must have loved gardening."

He pushed open the front door and gestured her in. "Actually, I planted them."

"*You* did?"

He grinned. "You can close your mouth now. I'm good for one or two things out of the sack. I used to help my mom with our yard in Connecticut."

"I'm sorry." Laine shook her head and smiled apologetically. Oops. She would have guessed he'd consider dandelions and ragweed the perfect landscaping. How could she not know this about him? She owed him what they agreed to in the train. To ditch her preconceived notions of who and what he was and to start fresh.

"Welcome home."

Laine nearly tripped over the threshold. Home? Her heart started pounding. He closed the door behind her.

Swish. Thunk.

For a second she thought of those horror movies

where the door creaks and then slams shut by itself, leaving innocents trapped in a haunted castle.

Grayson switched on the hall light and her fantasy vanished into pleasure.

A beautiful hardwood-floor hallway led them to a raised living room with sliding-glass doors looking out over a backyard too dark to see. Subtly hued Oriental rugs, a leather chair, brass table, glass, more dark wood, antique this and that, the room was stunning and made her all the more aware of how the furnishings in her apartment looked like college dorm stuff that had graduated to a fancier setting.

For a weird moment she felt as if she were seeing another part of him she'd never seen before, a part light-years older and more mature. As if he'd grown up and left her behind.

"You like it?"

"It's beautiful." She turned to find him standing behind her, hands on his hips, watching her with a curiously vulnerable expression, as if it mattered deeply what she thought. The feeling of being naive and young vanished into an urge to cross the few steps between them, take his face in her hands and kiss away any worry.

So why didn't she?

"The kitchen's this way." He gestured toward another doorway, up three more steps to a modern, beautifully designed kitchen, with glass-fronted cabinets and a granite-topped island. Copper pots hung from the ceiling on a round iron rack; a braid of garlic cloves and a wreath of dried herbs had been thoroughly plundered—ingredients, not just decoration. He cooked now, too? A dining room was off to one side, more hardwood and an oval table with six chairs.

"Wow." She looked around some more, touching, letting her hand linger over the smooth-top stove, the cold, granite counters. She imagined him here every morning, making his breakfast, eating it alone at the table for six…and something shifted in her heart.

"I love this place." She met his eyes and smiled.

He nodded, still looking at her with an unfamiliar intensity.

A bubble of emotion welled up, closing her throat, making breathing difficult. She turned away, pretending to examine the glassware in the cabinet opposite her. What was the matter with her?

"Laine." Her whispered name was an endearment; he moved behind her, ran his hands down the length of her bare arms, entwined his fingers with hers, rested his forehead next to her temple. "I love you."

Shock cut off her breath at the very moment she most needed to take in a huge lungful.

In all the years they'd been together, he'd never, ever…nothing like that had ever come out of his mouth.

She found herself gripping his fingers and forced herself to relax before she hurt him. What should she say? She wasn't ready. She couldn't say it back.

Damn it, she had to say *something*. "I—I'm…"

He pulled away. "Come see the upstairs."

Laine turned, eyes lowered, and registered the hand he held out to her. Oh, God, had she hurt him?

"It's okay." His voice was gentle. "You weren't expecting it."

She nodded, feeling like the world's biggest jerk. He said he loved her, something she would have given any appendage to hear him say in college or in any of the years after, and she'd totally choked.

What was the matter with her?

She followed him up hardwood stairs painted white on the vertical surface, up to an attractive guest room and another tidy but cluttered bedroom he used as an office. Closet, then bathroom and, at the end of the hall, the king-size-bed-dominated, equally tastefully decorated master bedroom.

He strode to the center of the room, arms out wide, devilish grin on his face. If she'd devastated him by not responding to his declaration, he was giving no sign.

"And this, Laine, is known as the Pit of Passion."

She burst out laughing. "Oh? And how many women have died of multiple orgasms here?"

"None." He shook his head mournfully. "But not for lack of trying to lure them in."

She laughed again, knowing that if he'd wanted a woman here, he would have had no trouble finding one. The thought made her feel giddy and solemn all at the same time. He loved her. He'd opened his mouth and said so. Even Grayson the Salesman wouldn't have said that unless he really meant it.

Maybe it would take time before it hit her. Right now she didn't feel much more than giddy and solemn and a little freaked. Which was hardly the melt-into-his-arms-as-the-music-swells joy she should be feeling.

Damn it.

"You okay?" He moved toward her, took her shoulders and gazed intently into her face.

She nodded.

"You're not in shock or anything?"

She giggled and hunched her shoulders, shaking her head, nervous around him as if this was their first date. What was it about being in his house that made her so on edge where she'd been so bold and so sure of him and of herself in the train?

Maybe being nervous was good. Maybe it meant she was taking the starting-over thing seriously. Except she didn't know many men who said, "I love you" on the first date. She was about to let out another stupid giggle when he leaned forward and kissed her, a long, sweet kiss that made first-time thrills race around her body. She wanted to wrap her arms around his neck, but couldn't seem to do more than awkwardly clutch his shoulders.

He pulled back, smiled, then leaned forward again, using the tip of his tongue to outline her lips in a slow, sensual circle.

Her sex started to heat. This she could understand. This was familiar territory. And being back in it hit like a relief and a loss at the same time.

He put his arms around her, gathered her close and kissed her again, but where she expected their usual explosion of passion to go off any second, there was only more of that consciousness-stealing sweetness, kiss after kiss after kiss.

She managed to unclutch his shoulders, to get her arms around him, and then gradually, like a slow slide into sleep, her whole body started to let go. She couldn't explain it better than that, couldn't really understand, but she left her tense Laine persona behind, shed it like too-tight clothes, and gave herself over to this immersion into Grayson's lips and body until she almost seemed to…disappear.

Oh, no.

She tried to pull back, but he kept her in a firm hold. Kissed her patiently until she relented, let herself go again, drifted into a blissful state where she was no longer whole in herself and no longer cared.

His fingers touched her back; he unzipped her dress, letting his palms linger on her bare skin, searching for the bra she wasn't wearing, hadn't wanted to wear.

The dress fell to the floor, leaving her suddenly naked, and her blissful state melted into insecurity in front of this man who had seen her naked hundreds of times. He swept her up into his arms, laid her tenderly in the center of his enormous bed and took off his own clothes, deliberate and unhurried.

"Come here." He stripped off the bedspread while she wriggled out of the way, leaving the sheet and a light blue cotton blanket. She slid under the covers and he joined her so they faced each other.

"Hi."

"Hi." She tried to grin, but she felt too much emotion and saw too much reflected in his eyes.

He pulled her close. "I couldn't wait to feel you this way in my bed, to feel your skin against me."

She nodded into his shoulder, uneasy, unsure. Why couldn't she relax?

He pushed the blanket off her shoulder, traced the line of her arm with gentle fingers.

"You are so soft." He bent forward, kissed the line he'd just caressed, then moved his kisses along the curve of her waist up to the side of her breast. "So beautiful."

Laine took in an awed breath. He'd never said things like that before, never taken his time like this, not with this deliberate tenderness. She'd never needed him to, she was always hot and ready in record time. What was he doing?

She forced herself to let the breath go. Took in another. Repeated the process.

"What's the matter?" He even noticed her breathing tonight.

"You're…different."

"Different better?"

"Well, yes. You've never been so slow, or said things like that before."

"I've always been thinking them, Laine." He kissed between her breasts, then traced one finger lightly across each tip. His touch was so gentle, so reverent, so far from his usual welcomed assault on her body.

He leaned forward and took her nipple into his mouth; she braced herself for the nip of his teeth.

Grayson pulled back and chuckled. "No pain today. Just pleasure. Just us."

She nodded, roused herself from her trancelike paralysis and threaded her fingers through his wonderful dark hair. This was what she wanted, what she'd dreamed of. She could do this.

He kissed her again, his tongue gradually taking part in the kisses until she moved tight against him, driven by a deep need to be closer, and discovered that he was exercising a hell of a lot of self-control with all this patience. Under the blanket he was hugely hard already.

She pressed her sex against his erection, expecting her arousal to take off, but strangely, didn't feel the urgent need to have him inside her, not the way she usually did, the way she had even in the train. Somehow this kissing, this gentle, slow touching was drugging her, pushing her to a place where the orgasm seemed secondary.

He turned her onto her back, peeled back the covers and stroked her—throat to breast, breast to waist, waist to stomach, letting his fingers trail over each inch, occasionally leaning over to taste what he'd touched.

She lay quietly, absorbed in the delicious sensations, understanding that this was a gift he wanted to give her, that her turn to pleasure him would come soon.

He brushed his hand down, over her pubic curls, touched her sex lightly, then moved back to her abdomen, leisurely sweeps over her breasts and back down to tease her sex again.

Laine took in a deep breath. She wanted to keep the relaxation, keep the dreamy pace going, but his warm hands in the cool room touching her so intimately were making her a little crazy.

"Relax. Close your eyes."

She closed them, gave herself over to his expert caresses, then the sudden wet warmth of his tongue between her legs.

"Mmm." She lifted her hips, reached for his head.

"Lie still."

She obeyed, forcing herself to relax. He took his time, tasting her, using the slippery slide of his tongue to increase her pleasure.

She waited for the excitement to carry her away—this time surely it would—but the fiery wild rush she always felt with him didn't come. This arousal was more peaceful; she felt somehow more aware of Grayson, of his grace, his masculinity, his patient loving skill.

And suddenly she wanted to give that all back.

She sat up, pulled his head away; their eyes met and she smiled, a smile that was more innocence than the seduction she intended. Whatever they had between them was more powerful tonight than it had ever even come close to being.

"My turn." She put a hand to his chest and pushed.

He grinned and lay back. She touched him, massaging, caressing everywhere, the same devoted way he'd touched her. Then she lowered her head to taste him, to take his erection inside her mouth, long, patient strokes instead of her usual triple-X frenzy to devour him.

Her eyes closed; she explored him with her tongue and lips, concentrated on his taste, on the smooth, hot feel of his skin, on the way he moaned and shifted, how his breathing showed what he liked best—everything she'd done so many years ago to learn him, but tonight it seemed she was doing for the very first time.

The table next to his bed rattled; she heard the crinkle of a foil packet.

"Laine."

She looked up at him, feeling warm and dreamy and safe.

"Let me make love to you."

That was all he said, but she understood this sex wouldn't be about power and control, about gymnastics and challenges and new positions and methods.

She quelled the sudden rush of nerves. It would be good for them. They needed this.

"Yes."

She moved alongside him, stroking his magnificent chest as he rolled on the condom. He moved over her and she parted her thighs, reached down and guided him into the place he knew well enough to reach on his own.

He entered her, filled her as he always had, but this time there was no pumping, no laughter, no loud moans or giddy shrieks. Grayson wrapped his arms around her and started to move.

They probably made love all night long, she didn't know. But after he started his slow rhythm, time seemed to stop. Once in a while he'd lift his head, look down at her with unspeakable tenderness, and join their lips in a slow, sexy kiss.

She wanted to come and she didn't, she was about to and she wasn't ready yet. Everything seemed suspended in the push-and-pull emotion of their physical sharing.

"Laine," he whispered.

"Mmm?" She trailed her fingers down his back, felt his muscles bunch and release as he thrust.

"Move in with me."

Adrenaline shot through her; she stilled her hands. "What?"

He pushed in, pulled out, did it again. "I want to live with you."

"You—" She struggled for words and thoughts. Live with him? Here?

He increased his rhythm, started thrusting harder. She grabbed his shoulders, lifted her hips in response to the increased stimulation, which was making her want to come *now* except she was blown away by his demand. Why on earth hadn't he waited until they were done?

"What...kind of time is this to ask me?"

He drove harder, faster. "The perfect time."

"You couldn't have…waited until I wasn't so…distracted?"

He shook his head, eyes half closed, body working. "Now or never."

"Oh, no." She wiggled and pushed him until he let her roll them over so that she was on top. Was that what all this sweet seduction was about? To get her in a place where she'd agree to anything he asked?

"Tell me." She grabbed his wrists and pinned them over his head, used the forward thrust of her weight as ballast to help lift her hips up and down over his erection, feeling a thrilling rush of familiar power. "Why did you wait to ask me until just now?"

He shook his head. "I won't talk. You can't make me."

She laughed and pumped him harder. "Why now?"

He pulled his hands free, put them to her waist to help her up-and-down motion with his powerful arms, and thrust up into her with more force. "Because…Laine."

"Yes?" She panted the word, riding him, stretching her arms up and letting them fall behind her head, elongating her body, balancing with the strength in her thighs.

He gave an ecstatic groan, watching her, thrusting inside her. Then his face froze, his eyes closed, his lips parted over a sudden inrush of air, and she felt him contracting inside her.

She smiled. This was what they did best. Wild abandon, sexual frenzy. She dragged her hand up his chest and mercifully waited until most of his orgasm passed before she asked again.

"Tell me."

"For God's sake, give me a second. That was amazing."

"Okay, okay." She counted one-Mississippi. "How about now?"

He growled and flipped her over, keeping them joined, then he brushed the hair off her face and smiled, touching her lips with a gentle finger. "I've been thinking about it for a while. I only just got up the nerve to ask you."

"Oh." Her giggles died. She lay there, bewildered, aroused, confused; he started to move again, slowly— the man could still go all night.

"Grayson, I don't…really. I mean—"

"Shh. I've had a lot of time to think about this. You take some now."

She nodded, brain whirling, body slowly being consumed in a fiery response to his flawless knowledge of her physical needs. "Okay. But—"

"No buts. Think about it later." He moved his lips close to her ear. "Because right now I'm going to make you come."

She moaned, the thrill of his words pushing her closer to her climax. God, he turned her on. He kept the rhythm steady, knowing the patterns she liked, the rhythms she responded to. Steady, steady, then raised himself off her, pulled halfway out and made tiny thrusts, only an inch or so with each one.

She cried out, reached for completion, strained, clutched his solid biceps. She was so damn close, so damn close, so damn close…

He knew the precise moment, pushed back in to the hilt one more time. She started the explosion, the burning crest, over the edge into blissful contractions, while he drove harder, the way she loved it while she was coming.

This was enough. This feeling, this excitement, this erotic charge.

The rest she'd deal with, yes. But not now, not now.

Some other time.

11

From: Laine Blackwell
Sent: Monday
To: Angie Keller; Kathy Baker
Subject: Everything Changes

Weeeeeell…

What a difference a day makes. Last Friday night Grayson asked me to move in with him. I swear I almost swallowed my tongue. Where did that come from? Who is this unmasked man?

I know, it's not funny. Believe me, I'm not laughing.

The thing is, I couldn't answer him. Not yes, not no. I was so surprised and so…I don't know. And this is what I always said I *wanted* from him. What I always found fault with him for not providing—stability, commitment, blahblahblah. Now I think it might be *me* that's the problem. I know, it sounds so strange.

I came home midafternoon after spending two total slug days in bed with him, eating junk food, having sex, watching TV and just hanging. And we could have gone kayaking, one of my favorite things to do! But did I want to move? Or do anything that would take him out of touching range? Nnnnnooooooo.

How pathetic is that?

One weekend together and I'm turning into my mom. Can frumping around in curlers and a bathrobe be far behind? Giving up graduate school? Having a million babies and never leaving the house again?

It's not what I want. It's not the way I want to be. Love always makes me that way, pathetic and clingy and insipid. Beat me, whip me, whatever you want, if I love you I'll keep coming back for more.

Help! I think I need rescuing. Or advice. Tell me to tell him no. Or tell me to tell him that I need the rest of my summer to think about it. Maybe commitment and journalism will go together nicely. Whadya think?

Something's gotta give. I can feel myself sliding into that place where I'd eat live bugs if it would make him happy.

I. So. Do. Not. Want. To. Go. There. Again.

What do I do? I love the guy like crazy.

Confusedly,

Laine

"SO WHAT'S UP, my man?" Ted glanced over at Grayson. The two of them had just finished stretching and were out for a Tuesday afternoon jog around the reservoir in Central Park. "I have a feeling you didn't invite me to join you because you wanted to watch me pass out after a quarter mile."

"Sure I did." Grayson smiled. He didn't have a whole lot of energy himself. Hadn't for the past few days, since he'd put Laine on a train for New York last Sunday and had the weird feeling it was the beginning of The End.

How could he explain her deer-in-the-headlights reaction to moving in with him? The rest of the weekend had been great, as long as he kept everything about the present. One mention of the past or, God forbid, the future, and she'd stiffen, go quiet, force the smiles and laughter.

"Let me guess. It's something to do with…" Ted waved his hand in circles as if he was attempting to conjure up the truth. "Ohhhh, I'm guessing…Laine."

"Yeah." Why bother denying it? He enjoyed spending time with Ted, but this time he wasn't afraid to admit he needed advice.

"So what's the problem?" Ted was already starting to sweat.

"I asked her to move in with me."

"She turned you down?"

"Not outright."

"Skittish, then."

"She nearly stopped breathing, does that count?"

"Hmm." Ted swerved to go around a shapely power walker, giving her long, hardworking legs a lingering glance. "You know…Nora went through something like that. But with her it was fear I would cheat on her."

"Can't blame her."

"No, I couldn't. Women know you can *say* anything. It's the doing that counts." He blew in and out a few times. "And unless and until you build up that trust…words don't mean squat."

Grayson nodded. "Like the golden triangle of sales."

"Golden who?"

"Triangle." Grayson sketched one in front of him with his hands. "Forty percent of a salesman's process toward success is gaining the potential client's trust. Thirty percent is finding out what the client needs. Twenty percent is the actual presentation where you propose to meet those needs, and a mere ten percent is the closing of the deal."

"And most people make their mistake…"

"Thinking the presentation is the most important part."

"Okay, go with that. Does she trust you?"

Grayson shrugged. Short of her saying, "Oh by the way, dear, I trust you now," how could he tell? But he'd more than answered her "And then what?" question so she had to realize he was not in this for the short haul. "I think she does. Yes."

"Second point." Ted held up two fingers and wiggled his eyebrows, panting hard now. "Are you addressing her…needs?"

"She's satisfied, yes." Grayson grinned. "Frequently."

Ted chuckled. "How about her other needs?"

"Other needs?" Grayson put on a confused expression. "They have other needs?"

"D'oh." Ted smacked himself in the forehead, which had turned a sweaty shade of red. "I think, yeah."

"I'm trying. I'm better than I used to be, but she's still wary. I can't figure it out."

"Hmm." Ted started to lag behind, blowing like a horse. "I think…I know…what the problem…is."

"Yeah?" Grayson turned to jog backward and regarded him with cautious optimism. "What's that?"

"I'm about to have a heart attack."

Grayson rolled his eyes and dropped to a walk. "Better?"

"Whoa." Ted stopped altogether, bent over, hands on his knees, and panted. "You do this to yourself on purpose?"

"Every day. Or every other."

"You are one sick puppy, my man." He hauled himself upright, stretched his back and reluctantly started walking. "Well, here's the thing. If Laine is anything like Nora was, she wants the whole shebang up front."

"And which shebang would that be?"

"The ring."

Grayson nearly tripped over his own feet. Adrenaline started pumping through his body. "The ring?"

"That's what the problem was for her. After we'd been dating a year, I asked her to move in with me, she was way lukewarm, like, 'Gee, thanks, but I'm late going home to stick hot pins in my eyes.'"

"Ooh." Grayson sucked in air through his teeth. "I lived the same reaction."

"It nearly killed me. I thought I'd offered her the moon in a bottle and it wasn't enough until she got the damn jewelry. Like what difference did that make in how I felt about her?"

Grayson lifted an eyebrow. "I assume you're asking rhetorically?"

"Yeah." Ted ran his fingers through his sparse hair and walked with his hands clasped behind his head. "So I cursed, screamed, tried to put my fist through a wall, went on a drinking rampage, did shots of tequila until my eyeballs crossed. Then I went home, passed out, woke up in my own puke and thought, 'Hmm, marriage might be okay.'"

Grayson burst out laughing, that strange electric thrill still going strong. "That's all it took?"

"Okay, maybe it wasn't that simple." Ted grinned and wiped his face on his shirt. "I did a lot of soul searching. Stopped going out, stayed home and read some books on marriage, all of which scared me shitless. But in the end I realized it was what I wanted. I still had no idea what it would be like—I guess no one really does—or how I'd handle it, whether I was even cut out for it. There are still times I miss being single." The power walker caught up to them and passed; Ted gave her firm, pumping rear the look of a child to forbidden candy and sighed. "But hell, for all intents and purposes I wasn't free anyway, being that crazy about Nora. And not proposing meant I would lose her. It wasn't worth the risk."

Yes. Grayson squinted into a cooling breeze sweeping over the water. He knew exactly what Ted meant, and it was shaking him up good. Not because the idea of marrying Laine was scary. But because it wasn't. The more Ted talked, the more the idea excited him. He felt as if he were standing on the edge of a bridge, bungee cord tied tight, nearly ready to jump. A new adventure, like the ones Laine was forever trying. "So you asked her."

"Yup. I bought the ring, a bouquet of her favorite flowers, showed up at her house, threw them at her and said, 'Okay, you win.'"

Grayson stopped walking. "No way."

"Nah." Ted waved him to catch up. "But I'll tell you, once we were engaged I couldn't see what the hell I'd ever been afraid of. It was an awesome time, man. And for all the rough spots, it keeps getting better."

"Christ, you sound like a commercial."

"I know, I know." Ted grimaced. "I'm whipped. But I'm also happy. You and Laine should come over for dinner some night. Meet Nora and the kids."

"Thanks, I'll mention it to her." He shot Ted a grin, imagining the domestic scene in which Laine truly belonged to him. Awesome. "You ready to run again?"

Ted sent him a plaintive look. "Do I have to?"

"Yup."

They ran several more yards, watching ducks bobbing on the surface of the reservoir.

"So, how's business?"

"Hopeful." Grayson shortened his stride to keep from sending Ted into another collapse. "I got an appointment to see the director of marketing at Browning Systems."

"Excellent." Ted held up his hand for a high-five. "How did you get in there?"

"CEO is a friend of Laine's. She went out with him once and the guy started sending her huge bouquets of flowers every week, so they stayed in touch."

"Wanted into her pants, huh."

Grayson wiped his arm across his forehead. "That's what I thought. But he says he just wanted to make her happy."

"What?" Ted turned to stare incredulously and had to do an emergency evasive maneuver to keep from running over a middle-aged jogger barely stumbling along. "What a wussy."

"Hey!" The jogger gave Ted the finger and let loose a string of pure New Yorkese.

"Not you. Chill out." Ted shook his head and turned back to Grayson. "Go on."

"So the four of us had dinner last Friday—Laine set him up with her friend, Judy—and I have a meeting there tomorrow."

"Fabulous. And the bouquets?"

"I guess he'll be sending them to Judy now."

"So you get the flowers now for Laine."

"Oh, for—" Grayson sighed. He'd about had it up to here with flowers. "I thought love was about never saying sorry, not trips to the florist."

"Buy her favorites—what are they?"

"How the hell should I know?

"What?" Ted took one look at Grayson's face and lifted his hands in despair. "Okay, never mind. Buy any old bunch. Then get a ring—they like honking diamonds best—show up at her door and you're in. You got your trust factor taken care of, you're satisfying her needs, you have a beautiful presentation and all it takes is the ten percent of her saying 'I do' to close the deal."

Grayson shook his head in amazement. This was twice now that Ted had brought up the subject of proposing to Laine. He still wasn't freaking. In fact he was starting to get seriously pumped over the picture of him offering the ring, declaring his love, waiting for the look on her face... If anything would put her doubts to rest, a proposal would.

He grinned. "You make it sound so simple."

"It is simple, my man." Ted slapped him on the back. "That's the damn beauty of it."

Grayson nodded. A chuckle escaped him even though he couldn't think of any reason to chuckle. He was flying. He'd think about it, just to be sure, try the idea on for size to see how it fit for the next few days. He already knew Laine was the woman for him, he'd probably always known, even in college—maybe that was why he'd panicked so badly when she said she loved him, since he wasn't mature enough to handle emotion that deep.

And last Friday, ten years later, when he finally told Laine he loved her, it had been one of the most thrilling and weirdly freeing moments of his life. He hadn't planned to tell her, hadn't known until the words had left his mouth that he was going to say them. But at that moment, with Laine finally in his house, a rare decoration that belonged there so well, the words had come out effortlessly. And once given, he didn't want them back.

He put on a burst of speed, shot past Ted, doubled back and did it again, light, euphoric, bursting with energy and purpose.

Right now he'd bet a marriage proposal to Laine would feel exactly the same way.

From: Angie Keller
Sent: Tuesday
To: Laine Blackwell; Kathy Baker
Subject: My my my

Uh-oh. We have gotten our delightful little ass into trouble here. You have betrayed your summer, you Delilah! You're supposed to be getting laid, not falling in love. As my mom used to say, 'You've gone and pooped in your own bait bucket.' And now you see how messy and unrewarding it is? Me, I kissed Carlo at the door last night and came inside where I could pass gas and let my stomach hang out in peace, watch the channels *I* want to, thank you most awfully much, and eat dinner straight out of the ice-cream carton. I don't have to launder, nag or pick up after anyone but little ol' me, and then only when I feel like it or run out of underwear. *What are you thinking?*

Half-kidding aside, you have it bad for this guy, darlin'. Not to sound like that Nervous Nellie, Kathy, but be careful. Remember the chase theory? The further we up the stakes to make them prove they're here to stay, the higher those man-ponies jump. But it's the same as it ever-lovin' was. Once you stop treating them like shit, once you feel secure and become sweet, loving and attentive instead, it's all over.

Been there, been dumped by that. Repeatedly.

If it was me, which I know it ain't, I'd protect myself. Just say no to living together. Stay in charge and watch him grovel after you until death do you part.

Angie has spoken.

God bless.

From: Kathy Baker
Sent: Tuesday
To: Laine Blackwell; Angie Keller
Subject: Wow

Oh gosh, Laine! What are you thinking? Do you have any idea how madly in love with you he must be to voluntarily give up his freedom? It's every girl's fantasy to get the guy who can't commit to commit to her. You have that! This Man To Do stuff is fine, but let's face it, all of us are really looking for what you found—okay, except maybe Angie, the über-slut. ☺ Hi, Angie! (waving innocently).

Move in with the guy. He's serious this time. I guarantee it. You don't have to be afraid anymore.

Kathy

P.S. CARLO, Angie? I thought it was David. DAMN you get around, woman. I hope you're smothering these guys in latex first.

LAINE HUNG UP the kitchen phone after Judy's call and huffed an unsatisfying breath of too-warm apartment air. Lovely. Today's regularly scheduled programming, Saturday lunch at Clark's, cancelled again, this time due to love of Ben.

The same phenomenon was happening everywhere, like some B-movie horror plot. Perfectly sane, rational, independent women got a sniff of testosterone and their entire universe dwindled to a penis with legs attached.

Including Laine.

She pulled her hair into a low ponytail and wrapped it in the scrunchy she had around her wrist. This moment of disgust called for a snack of some kind. Sweet? Salty? Crunchy? Chewy? Too hot to think. She ambled to the cabinet and stared at her impressive snack selection, even the slow movement causing a fresh breakout of perspiration. Only 10:00 a.m. and getting hotter tomorrow.

Forget high electricity bills. She shut the cabinet door on her indecisiveness, moved around the apartment, closing windows and turning on the air-conditioner, her skin eager to receive the first breaths of cooling air. Dragging herself back to the kitchen cabinets, she selected a bag of mini-marshmallows. Perfect. Squishy. Without substance. About how her brain felt.

Now. What to drink? She rummaged in the refrigerator, enjoying the frosty air misting out into the warm room, considered a beer, but couldn't handle the implications of drinking this early, nor imagine the taste combined with marshmallow. Diet soda then.

There. She was set. Another glorious, productive, nutritional morning.

She shuffled back to her room clutching the soft, sticky plastic bag, and flopped down onto her bed. Three times already she'd picked up the phone to call Grayson. Three times she'd put it down. Excuse me, could she not get through a morning now without him?

They'd spent the night together twice more since the weekend in Princeton. Two blissful nights. He was becoming more and more the Stepford Boyfriend, never missing an opportunity to touch her, compliment her, kiss her. No more predator, no more conflict or challenge. It was all so…easy and natural between them now. At least when she let herself go and enjoyed it. Which, damn it, was becoming easier and easier to do. Only now, in the cold, harsh—okay, *hot,* harsh light of reality, did she start to realize where she was headed.

She popped a marshmallow into her mouth and savored the foamlike sweetness. Look at her. Here it was, July 14, halfway through her fabulous summer, and all she'd managed to accomplish was—

She lifted her head, gulped the marshmallow and shot to a sitting position. July 14. Bastille Day and Mom's birthday. Damn. She hadn't gotten her mother a card, a gift, nothing. She'd been so wrapped up in Grayson...

And there, in a nutshell, was her point.

The phone next to her bed rang as she was about to grab it, and she nearly jumped out of her skin.

"Laine, it's Mimi. Have you called Mom?"

"I was just about—"

"Damn it, Hank, the baby's in the cat food. *No,* I am on the phone." Her sister's voice became indistinct as she unsuccessfully tried to muffle the tirade at her husband. "I work my ass off around these kids 24/7, I have to ask permission to take a *shower,* for Pete's sake. You can get your ass away from the TV for thirty seconds and get Nathan out of the damn cat food."

Laine's stomach started to churn. Love was a many-splendored thing.

"Sorry, Laine." Mimi's exasperated voice came back clearly on the line. "I swear, he thinks his own life should just mosey along as usual, like the four kids in the house have nothing to do with him."

Laine wasn't touching that one. "How are you feeling?"

"Horrible. Throwing up all day, I swear this is my last kid. I don't care how many he wants, it's me who has to deal with them, and this is absolutely... *Hank,* for God's sake, get this baby out of the 9-Lives before he starts meowing. I gotta go, ~~Laine.~~ Call Mom, she was bitching at me that she hadn't heard from you yet."

"It's still morning." Laine scowled and lifted her ponytail off her neck to catch more fast-cooling air.

"I know, I know. Look, I have to go—uh, how are you doing?"

"I'm fine." Laine sighed. She and her sister used to be so close. Best friends. Until Mimi met Hank and went down the love toilet. "Just fine."

"Good. Why don't you come out here? Once I'm over this morning sickness I could use a girls' night out like we used to do. Except virgin margaritas for me."

"I'd love that."

"Damn it, Hank! Okay, Laine, stay in touch, love you."

Click.

Laine punched off her phone and grimaced. She remembered Mimi on her wedding day, gazing at Hank as if he was Mr. Universe, her dream man, the answer to all her prayers.

And now look.

Did this have to happen? As Laine fell more and more in love with Grayson, was she hurtling toward a head-on, heart-smashing collision with misery and resentment?

She wrinkled her nose, dialed her mother and prepared her Happy Daughter Voice to avoid being cross-examined.

"Hi, Mom! Happy birthday!"

"Aw, thank you, baby, you're sweet to have remembered. I was just telling your father that we should call. Want me to call you back?"

"Of course not."

"You sure?"

"Yes, I'm sure. How are you celebrating today?" Laine rolled her eyes. As if there was any question.

"Your father and I are going to Manitero's for lasagna, it's so good there, and then we'll come home to eat a cheesecake from Densik's, plain with cherry topping, you know us, same as we always do. Your father doesn't like to try new places, he likes to know exactly what he's getting.''

"That sounds nice, Mom." She pictured the two of them, dressed in their "going out" clothes, sitting at the restaurant in their customary silence, conversation apparently having dried up years ago. "What else is going on?"

"Your father bought a new lawn mower last week. I told him we didn't need a new lawn mower, there was nothing wrong with our old lawn mower, but you know how men are. So I said to him, well if you can have a new lawn mower, I need a new dishwasher, since we bought this one practically right after we got married, and…''

Laine slumped backward onto her mattress. Oh, this was so not what she needed right now—dual pictures of domestic non-bliss. And hadn't they all started out dewy-eyed and hopeful, hands and hearts as one, sure their love was so special, so profound, so deep, that nothing would ever change it?

Except boredom.

And stress.

And familiarity breeding contempt.

She listened to the rest of Mom's complaints and mundane bits of gossip, exchanged a few stock phrases with her father, promised to come visit, hung up and rubbed her aching temples. She really, really, really didn't want to think about all this anymore. Not about love, not about getting serious. Not about any of it.

So.

She looked blankly around the room.

Now what? What was she going to do with this day?

She folded her legs up to her chest and rested her face on top of one knee so her nose squashed nearly flat. Since when did she ever have to ask herself that?

Since Grayson.

She hadn't practiced her tap routine all week. She'd dropped French; the language was beautiful, but *parlez*-ing was never going to be Laine's forte. Nor was pottery. None of the new cooking classes appealed. Men To Do were out for obvious reasons, and even with Grayson, she'd rather stay home than party all night on the town. As for skydiving, something she'd wanted to do her whole life, Grayson seemed uncomfortable with the idea of her hurtling toward the earth with only nylon for protection, and quite honestly, she hadn't ever really come to terms with the terror bound to be involved.

So guess what? She'd given that up, too.

Love was bad for her. It was just bad. She'd started this summer absolutely flying. Every day was one joy after another. Then Grayson had come along and she'd begun the slow decline into depression, uncertainty, anxiety, immobility.

Instead of bouncing joyously in and out of Men To Do beds, she was lying here alone on hers, lonely, anxious, no longer happy being anywhere except in Grayson's company.

She'd gone from being a whole person to a half.

Worse, the calls today to her mom and sister cemented everything she'd been worrying about, all the things she'd spent her life wanting to avoid. Would she someday resent Grayson? Blame him for any and all unhappiness she encountered? Fight with him all day long? Or settle into such dull routines that she could predict what would happen every single day for the rest of her life?

Argh!

The phone rang again. She gave it a wary, sidelong look before picking it up. What now?

"Hey."

Mmm. She smiled just hearing his voice, wanting immediately to crawl through the line and to wrap herself around him, make him swear he'd never find her boring or annoying. "What are you doing?"

His deep chuckle came over the line. "Thinking about you. What are you doing?"

"The same." The words came out in not quite a tender drawl as his, but slightly sad, as if she was already mourning the death of their relationship. She hoped he hadn't picked up on it.

"Everything okay?"

He had. "Everything's fine."

"Are you ever going to tell me what's bugging you?"

She laughed, feeling a sudden wave of guilty panic. Yeah, was she ever? She had to, she owed it to him. But how could she tell someone she loved that she was actually frightened of the intimacy and commitment she thought she'd always wanted?

Probably just open her mouth and say it, right?

She opened her mouth. "Nothing's bugging me."

Ugh. The sick feeling in her stomach grew sicker. She was lying to the man she loved. She needed to come clean with him about her fears. Instead, she had a sudden urge to book a flight to New Orleans, hang out on Bourbon Street and immerse herself in debauchery until she was too old to debauch anymore.

Except it wouldn't be any fun without Grayson.
Help.

"I'm coming in to see you tonight."

The cold wave of panic turned into the warmth of pleasure, except for the channel bell clanging a warning. He was announcing, not asking. Shouldn't she be upset? "I'm glad."

She *was* glad. Crazy glad. Too glad.

"I'll bring Chinese takeout. Mu shu pork for me, kung pau chicken for you, an order of steamed dumplings and beer."

She twisted her lip, recognizing the menu as their standard anniversary meal, celebrating the night they got back together after the first breakup in college. Now she should be truly annoyed. She wasn't. She was lying here delighted that they were already eating the same thing every year, just like her parents.

Calm down, Laine.

"Are you there?"

"Yes. It sounds wonderful."

He chuckled. "Trust me. This evening will be much more than wonderful."

She smiled at the suggestive tone and pulled her hair loose from the scrunchy. "All evenings with you are more than wonderful."

"See you at seven."

"At seven." Which yes, happened to be a convenient time, but he could have asked, and that didn't bother her, either. She said goodbye and hung up.

Okay. Enough. She was being crazy. She loved him. He was coming over and she was damn happy about it and there was nothing wrong with that. People who loved each other were supposed to want to be together. In the days and weeks ahead, she would come to trust him more and more, work on herself so she could share her fears with him and tell him she loved him, too, which he certainly deserved to hear, even though he must know it was true.

And most of all, she needed to learn to ignore that the more perfect he was, and the closer they got, and the more she lost herself in loving him again...the more she wanted to run away.

12

LAINE LAY BACK on her bed, pulled the stocking slowly, carefully, up her leg and hooked the banded top into the metal and rubber fastener, smiling in satisfaction when she imagined Grayson's face catching sight of her getup.

Right now she was wearing a black lace bustier, black lace garter belt and black stockings. No panties, nor was she planning on any. Black, high-strappy sandals were next, then she'd put a nice dress over it all, so he wouldn't suspect.

After her morning mope, she'd figured out what she needed to feel more alive, more in control. A light sexual frolic to get away from all the angst, all the relationship issues, all the worry over what she needed, what he needed, what they needed, blahblahblah.

An evening of mindless fun, the way they used to spend time before they'd gotten so intense about everything. An old-fashioned seduction, or better yet, a game. Maybe female submission versus male dominance.

Or the other way around?

No. She didn't feel like a dominatrix tonight. Powerful, yes, but much more in the mood for kinky play going the other way.

Stockings fastened, she lay back on the bed, running her hands over her body, imagining Grayson's hands following the same path. Over her thinly-lace-covered breasts, down her stomach, then trailing the black lace of her garter and down between her legs. Her fingers felt warm on her air-conditioner-cooled skin, her sex responding with a burst of arousal. She wanted to be hot already when he showed up, not that she ever needed a whole lot of persuasion with Grayson.

Funny how she used to assume she was just built that way. Until Grayson moved to Chicago, she'd dated a few other guys—Jim, Carl, Sam, Brad—she discovered with them she had to work to get horny, had to concentrate just to come. She and Grayson had something extraordinary going on in the sex department, and it was time to stop whining about the rest of it and to celebrate that fact.

Laine wrinkled her nose and pushed herself up on her elbows. Yeah, she said all that already. Too many repetitions and it would start sounding as though she was trying to convince herself.

She got off the bed, leaned forward and adjusted the bustier for maximum breast thrust, glancing at the clock next to her bed. Six fifty-five; he was usually pretty punctual.

Quick. She grabbed the scoop-necked, sleeveless, black-and-burgundy minidress from where it hung, freshly ironed, above the closet, pulled it over her head, stepped into the sandals and went over to the full-length mirror behind her door.

Perfect. She looked like someone who'd put on a fairly dressy dress to impress a new date. Combination sexual and innocent. The skirt flared slightly and did cool, swirling things when she walked; the rest clung in all the right places. Grayson would love what he saw when he walked in. And love what he couldn't see yet even more.

The door buzzer rang—four short, one long, two short, one long—followed by the sound of the apartment door unlocking and swinging open. Her heart gave a leap of excitement. Morse code for *S-E-X*. He was in the same mood she was.

"Hi, honey, I'm ho-o-me."

She laughed at his overly hearty "Father Knows Best" imitation and pitched her voice to a sugary croon loud enough for him to hear. "Hello, dear, how was work today?"

"Grueling," he boomed back. "When you're a man like I am a man, you know that a man's life is very…manly."

"Poor baby." She grinned and gave herself one last check in the mirror. "Dinner will be on the table soon. It's meat loaf, your favorite!"

"Oh, boy. Meat loaf!"

She heard him chuckle and the rustle-thud of a heavy brown paper bag hitting the counter. Her man had brought home the bacon.

A strange longing seeped into her mood; she could see her eyes growing wistful in the mirror.

Immediately she crossed them and made a face at her reflection. No more Donna Reed wanna-be, remember? Not to mention she didn't even like meat loaf.

Forget. Suppress. Regroup. Let the games begin.

She took a breath of anticipation, stepped out into the hallway, turned toward him and waited, legs spread in a strong stance, letting her face show what she expected from him: one night of sexual satisfaction, please.

At the other end of the hallway, Grayson looked over from the bag he was unloading onto her kitchen counter. All movement stopped except for the slow smile that spread across his handsome, familiar, wonderful face.

"Hi."

"Hi." She let her voice come out low and throaty, reached down, took hold of the hem of her dress and slowly lifted it. His gaze dropped to the tops of her stockings and the garter, then wandered around the exposed lines of her thighs.

She lifted the skirt higher, carefully maneuvering her hands closer together, so a swath of material stayed draped over her sex. There she stopped, and put on an expression of open challenge.

He still stared at her legs, hands clutching a white cardboard container of Chinese takeout. Unexpected tension crept into her body. Would he play? He knew the game, knew the signals to start it. Or would he keep to this new path and insist on Stepford sex?

He raised his eyes to hers, then dropped them pointedly down to where the material still covered her.

"Show me the rest."

Laine's body relaxed into the river of relief running through it. He was going to play. Not until this second did she realize how tightly wound she'd been and how strangely fragile she felt. If he'd insisted on deep, slow, emotional sex, she probably would have shattered.

"No." She lifted her chin. "This is all you get."

His eyes flashed understanding and excitement before they darkened dangerously.

"I said, let me see."

She shook her head, keeping her ground, her breath ratcheting up a notch. They were so good like this. It was so exciting, so naughty, so right. Why did they ever try to be any other way?

He prowled down the hallway toward her, leisurely steps emphasizing the sexy swing of his powerful shoulders, eyes narrowed with the displeasure he played so well.

A foot away, he stopped. Laine kept still, face flushed, heart beating faster. She loved this game. For whatever sick, twisted reason, she did.

"I said, lift your skirt."

"No."

"Do it now."

"No."

He grabbed her shoulders and swung her back against the wall, taking his usual care not to hurt her, pinned her there and pushed his face close.

"Take your hands." His voice was a low growl; his warm breath mingled with her pretend-fear panting. "And pull up your skirt so I can see."

"No." She said the word in a mock-terrified sob and dropped her eyes.

His hands tightened on her shoulders. "One more chance."

"I won't do it."

He grabbed her chin, forced her to meet his cold stare. "Just remember, Laine. You asked for this."

She stared back, a little rattled. Something in his eyes and voice made it seem as if his words meant something outside of the game. As if he understood what she was avoiding by wanting to play tonight.

No, no. Crazy idea. He was just playing his part.

"I...didn't ask for anything." She tried to move out of his strong grip. "You're forcing me."

"Damn right." He pulled her roughly from the wall, turned her away from him, then yanked her back and held her tight with one iron arm. "You didn't do what I told you to do, so it's no longer about what you want. It's about what I choose to give you."

She cried out and struggled carefully, making sure not to get in his way. He unzipped his fly, his hands fumbled along her back; she heard the rough swish of cloth over skin.

"This is what you get." He bent her over, grabbed her hips and flipped up her skirt.

She heard his breath go in when he saw her lack of panties, an involuntary hiss of excitement he tried to disguise as disapproval. "Look at you."

"I was going to put some on," she protested pitifully. "You got here before I could."

"Liar." He caressed her bottom roughly with both hands, brought his thumbs together to trail down her center, up then down again, making her moan. "You're wet, too."

"I'm sorry," she whimpered. "Let me go."

"No. Stay there." He gave her rear a gentle slap. "Don't move unless I give the order."

"Yes. Okay. Yes." She heard the crinkling of foil and rolled her eyes, grinning. Damn condoms always spoiled the moment.

His arm came around her waist again; he leaned forward so his weight pressed on her, and she could feel his erection, hot and eager between her legs. "You feel that?"

"Yes." She wiggled as if to struggle, making sure her sex rubbed against him. "Get it away from me."

"It's going inside you."

"No!"

He grabbed her hips, pushed inside her and started pumping hard. She moaned and braced her arms against the wall to absorb the forward impact, waiting for her body to get carried away by the fantasy. "Please stop."

"No. You take it." He pumped her, lunging movements that made her whole body rock.

Her arm buckled and she bumped her head against the wall. "Ow."

"You all right?"

"Yes. Fine."

"Good." He kept thrusting; she moaned again. It felt damn good. It always felt damn good.

But something wasn't right. Something was missing, taking the edge off her excitement, and she had no idea what.

Maybe she was too tense? She took one hand off the wall, rubbed her clitoris for extra stimulation.

Without the support of both arms, her head bumped the wall again. He slowed his pace. Her back started to hurt.

"Um, Grayson?"

"Yes."

"I don't think it's going to happen."

"…Okay." He gave a few cool-down thrusts, held still, then pulled out gently, ran his hand along her back and helped her get upright. "Maybe we should have eaten first."

"Maybe." She turned, arms wrapped around herself, feeling disoriented and disappointed, almost near tears. "We could try that."

He nodded, pulled her close, kissed her, then gazed at her intently. "You sure that game was what you wanted?"

"Yes." She'd imagined this sex so carefully; it had started so well, they'd done variations of it before many times and enjoyed each one and each other tremendously. What had gone wrong?

"I didn't go too far?"

"Of course not." She shrugged and laughed nervously. "I feel totally safe with you."

Her words hung in the hallway and for one horrifying second she thought he was going to say something that would contradict her, bring it all up again. He had that about-to-say-something-important look. But she didn't understand what was happening, couldn't tell him what she was feeling, didn't want to talk about it.

To her relief, he kissed her again, moved away and grinned at her outfit. "You look unbelievable. I nearly had a heart attack when you came out of your room and lifted your skirt."

She smiled tightly. "I thought you'd like it."

"I did. I do. I will again." He wrapped an arm around her and propelled her toward her bedroom. "But I think there's something you need in here more than you need food."

"Um, my computer?"

He shook his head.

"A hairbrush?"

"Nope."

"Underwear?"

"Definitely not."

He led her up to her bed, turned her to face him and smiled tenderly. "Take off your clothes, get into bed and wait here."

Laine watched him leave the room with his confident, unhurried stride. Why did he want her to take her clothes off? She loved feeling this way, raunchy and sexual. And what was all this about? What was he going to get? He was making her nervous.

She shook her head and groaned in exasperation. She was turning into such a neurotic mess. He'd probably just bought a new sex toy. Or maybe he wanted to eat dinner in bed together, the way they used to, while watching old movies—only in this apartment her TV was in the living room.

She undressed, feeling vulnerable without her killer outfit, slid into bed and pulled the sheet up under her chin, trying to shake off the strange feeling of dread. Whatever he had up his sleeve, she hoped it didn't involve any more discussion of them moving in together. She hadn't made a decision yet and didn't want it to seem as though she wasn't taking the offer seriously or as though she was putting him off.

Even though she was.

He came back into the room, brandishing two beers. "I want to show you something amazing."

"Yes?"

"You see before you a beer bottle. Watch closely. Without an opener and with one quick effortless motion, it becomes…" He grabbed the cap and twisted it off. "An open beer bottle!"

She laughed and applauded. "You finally got it right."

"Yes." His eyes rested on her, darkening with an

emotion she didn't understand. "I think tonight I'm finally getting it right."

Her laughter died; she reached for her bottle. "So is this what you figured out I need? Alcohol?"

"Partly." He put his beer down on her computer and pulled off his clothes. She watched his incredible body emerge and the feeling of dread mixed with a weird, hollow sadness. "A bottle of beer, thou and some good conversation."

She sent him a pretend pout. "Not kinky sex?"

"Later." He retrieved his bottle, slid into bed and leaned back against the headboard. "After the mu shu pork comes the mu shu porking."

Laine slapped a hand over her mouth to avoid spitting beer, only letting laughter burst out after she managed to swallow. This was what she loved about him. How he made her laugh, took on each day and beat it into submission, made life into a fabulous comedy circus. So much more fun than all the intensity.

"So don't you want to know why I was into a celebration tonight?"

She glanced skeptically around the room. "Two beers in bed is a celebration?"

"Ha. Ungrateful wretch. I brought dinner, too."

She smiled. He knew she was teasing. She didn't have to go into any more explanation than that. "Okay, I'll bite. Why are we celebrating tonight, Grayson?"

"Two reasons."

"Yeeees?"

"One…" He puffed out his chest and took a swallow of beer. "Ben is going to hire Jameson Productions to do his projects, Web site, online sales, the whole picture. I close the deal next week."

"What?" She squealed and planted a long kiss on his cheek, as excited as if it had happened to her. "That's fabulous. That's amazing!"

"Yes indeedy." He lifted his hand and acknowledged applause from an invisible crowd. "I am the man."

Laine snorted and kissed him again. "That really is wonderful. The big client you've been hoping for."

"Yup." He clinked his bottle to hers. "And I have you to thank for that."

She shook her head. "*You* sold him."

"But you paved the way." He leaned over and joined their mouths together, a victory kiss that gave way to other slower kisses. The sweet, loving, drugging kind that made her want to surrender her soul to him.

She managed to pull back and take another swallow of beer, avoiding his quizzical gaze.

"Laine."

She braced herself. Oh, God, here it came. Why was he always wanting to surgically insert himself into her brain? She liked him better the old way.

Except, when he was the old way, she really...didn't.

"Are you going to tell me what's—"

"No." The word came out much louder and harsher than she expected. They blinked at each other, then he lifted his brows.

"Okay."

"I'm sorry." She grabbed a handful of hair and pulled it back off her face. "I don't know what's wrong with me."

"I think I do."

She snuck a nervous peek at him. "You do?"

He nodded and cleared his throat, looking suddenly less comfortable and confident. "And that's where we come to my second reason we'll be celebrating tonight.

"Okay." She nodded, feeling that sick guilt again. He was going to try to clinch them moving in together, and she hadn't gotten her soggy brain in gear to decide whether it was what she wanted. Times like these, when they were so easy and fun together, it was a no-brainer. She wanted him 24/7. But that was part of the problem. If she had him 24/7, where was the room for her?

"You know why I cheated on you in college, Laine?"

She blinked and turned her head to see his face. Why on earth was he bringing this up now? "You told me. You freaked out, didn't want marriage."

"That's partly true." He gave a humorless smile. "At that age, marriage means your life is over, dude."

She managed a nod, trying to block the voice shouting that was true at any age.

"But there's more than that." He paused, and she wasn't sure if he wanted a reaction or was nervous about what he had to say. Which made her even more nervous.

"What?"

"I've worked a lot of this out over the last few weeks. I know I don't open up enough, that I've been the cause of a lot of our problems. But this is a good speech. So here it comes."

Laine swallowed and fingered the label on her beer, wishing they could get back to the fun. She was suddenly and unaccountably petrified. "I'm listening."

"Back in college I was scared because of how much I loved you. I went from being a totally self-centered kid to a man, so vulnerable to one other person that it was almost like my life was being taken away. Like it belonged more to you."

Laine's focus sharpened on the bottle label. Little crinkly spider lines in the foil, little nicks in the edges. Yet her brain had taken firm hold of what Grayson was saying.

"Go on."

"I was too young to handle it, didn't even realize what was going on. All I knew was that the way you talked about marriage freaked me out."

Laine put her beer down and hunched forward. "What way?"

"You don't remember?"

"No," she whispered. The whole episode was a blur of confusion and pain.

"You said since I was graduating, it was time we started thinking about getting married, that your mother and sister had gotten married at that same age."

Laine winced. God, she'd been so programmed back then as to what life had to be like. "I'm sorry. I was…"

"This isn't about sorry, it's about understanding." He smiled and started stroking her hair. "I remember thinking it sounded like an oven timer had gone off and that's how you knew the turkey was done. It didn't seem to have anything to do with us or what we wanted. I reacted badly, I screwed up big-time, that part hasn't changed and I still feel like shit about it. But that's why it happened." He let out a breath as if he were relieved to have said his lines with no mistakes. "We haven't exactly had a history of top-drawer communication."

She laughed bitterly. "No."

"But no one has ever been able to measure up to what I feel for you. It's just that in those years after college, running away was always easier than dealing with it, because the feeling never got any less terrifying."

Laine's swallow made a loud silly sound in the room. Terrifying. That was about the size of it.

He stopped stroking her hair, leaned over the edge of the bed and rummaged for something on the floor. In a sudden clairvoyant flash of certainty, she knew what was down there and that it was much, much scarier than him wanting to move in with her.

"Laine." He sat up again and the expected velvet box in his hand made equal parts thrill and panic battle around her body. A low hum started in her ears; the scene turned dreamlike. "What's between us isn't going to go away, and now we have the power to change it for the better. Maybe I'll always be scared. Maybe it's just who I am. But I finally realized that no matter how scary this seems…" His voice dipped into husky emotion and he cleared his throat. "Nothing is scarier than the thought of not having you in my life forever."

The box opened in front of her swimming vision. A diamond, flanked by four tiny rubies in a twisted gold setting. Gorgeous. Stunning. She didn't want to see it.

He reached for her icy, limp hand. "Laine, of my heart, who makes me laugh, makes me hot, whose smile makes my day bright, whose legs could launch a thousand ships, I love you, will you marry me?"

He slid the ring on; it fit her perfectly, felt heavy and cold on her hand. She stared in disbelief, then up at his beautiful, hopeful face. Panic rose up in a tidal wave and threatened to choke her. Married. Gone. Disappeared. Tied to a house, pinned down by kids, turned permanently into this depressed, clingy half person who couldn't get motivated to do anything but moon after him and spread her legs.

"Laine?"

Tears spilled over onto her cheeks, she shook her head at the man she loved so much and reached to touch him with a shaking hand.

"I'm sorry, Grayson."

He turned to stone in front of her, this warm, beautiful, loving man. As if he'd stopped living at the sound of her words.

"I just can't."

13

From: Laine Blackwell
Sent: Sunday
To: Angie Keller; Kathy Baker
Subject: The Big One

Grayson asked me to marry him last night. Am I blushingly, blissfully engaged this morning? No. Not me.

I said no. I just can't. Not now. Marriage scares me to death. What if it ruins us? I couldn't bear that.

You should have seen his face. Like I killed him. I feel about six inches tall today. I can't stand that I hurt him.

I want to understand this and I want to get over the fear. More than anything, I want to make him happy. But if *I'm* not happy, I don't see how I can do that. We'd end up resenting the hell out of each other. Though it seems like most couples do anyway.

This whole Summer of Fun thing suddenly seems childish and superficial. Is that what I'm like?

Believe it or not, I got online and booked a ticket to Cincinnati. Running home to Mom.

How pathetic is that? But I feel somehow it will help me know what to do.

Grimly yours,
Laine

From: Angie Keller
Sent: Sunday
To: Laine Blackwell
Subject: Private to You

This is coming private e-mail to you, honey chile. Listen to Angie and listen good. You are not pathetic. You're just chicken shit. But this man loves you. You love him. Don't screw this up.

My secret—and if you ever, ever tell anyone, I will imprison you and force you to watch Lawrence Welk reruns for all eternity—is that I want to be in love. Deep-as-the-ocean, die-for-him in love. Like you are. Like he is.

I enjoy my Men To Do, honest. I really don't think I'm cut out for marriage. Multiple orgasms twice a week, sure. But many is the starry night I lie here wishing I was different.

You have a chance with this guy who adores you. Don't mess it up. Don't become like me, pushing thirty-five and still screwing boy-toys. You deserve better.

Do the right thing by this man. I know you will. You just have to look past the fear and take that first step.

Ah luvs yah, sugah.
God bless.
Angie

LAINE LOOKED OUT the window of the taxi from the Cincinnati airport to her childhood home in Hyde Park, watching the neat, orderly suburbs rush past. She felt older. Good older. Mature older. As if a lifetime of experience and knowledge had gradually fallen into her head in the past few months and become available to her in the last few days.

The start to her summer of fun had been so clear, so purposeful. Then Grayson had come back into her life and the whirlpool of the past few weeks changed everything, left her disoriented and gasping. Her glorious perspective on life had dwindled to him and to them. Period. She'd felt like a drowning victim, unable to latch on to anything to save herself. His proposal last week, instead of floating by like a miracle life raft, had dunked her under and squeezed off the last of her precious oxygen.

Now she was doing something positive. Something sane. Taking time to breathe deeply and well. Coming home to Ohio to see her mom and dad and sister. Trying to connect with who she was and what she wanted. Which was probably second nature to most people by her age. Leave it to her to spend her life in denial.

The taxi turned onto Berry Avenue. Laine leaned forward eagerly, craning for a glimpse of the familiar lemon-yellow homestead.

There it was! She paid the driver, shoved herself out of the cab, hopping a few times to free her other foot from the suitcase strap it tangled with. Home! She was home.

She crossed the narrow driveway toward the front stoop. How long since she'd been here? She'd spent last Christmas with friends at a ski wedding in Utah.

Her parents never came to the city; it intimidated the hell out of them. Had she really not seen them for over a year? Since the Christmas before last? Bad daughter, bad.

Now that she was back, she couldn't seem to remember why she'd put that distance between them. Maybe she really had grown up this summer. Ironically, Grayson was to thank for a lot of that, dragging her kicking and screaming into maturity. Or at least she hoped that's what this was.

The front door opened on her mother's smiling face, her hands held wide and aloft to embrace her much-taller daughter.

"Oh, my goodness, Laine, you are so beautiful. Howard, look how beautiful our daughter is."

"Hi, Mom." Emotion tightened her throat and she hugged her mother hard, inhaling her comforting mom-smell of 4711 cologne and Jergens lotion, surprised at how frail and small the familiar body felt.

"Dad." She hugged her father equally hard, noticing with a jolt that he was shorter than the last time she'd seen him. They were shrinking. Getting older. And she'd stayed away because…?

"Hey, Punkin. Welcome home." His deep voice was gruff; he held her tight even after her first move to break away.

"Come on in, dear." Mom patted her back, her soft, pale face flushed, hazel eyes glowing. "Dinner will be ready soon, you timed it perfectly."

They ushered her through the familiar olive-green hallway, her mom chattering about the new items in the house, the bargains she'd found, the projects her father hadn't yet completed. Two entire lives lived around this little house and yard in the 'burbs. Somehow that seemed calm and real, and not quite worthy of Laine's usual scorn. Who was she to judge? Look where her own choices had gotten her.

"Howard, take her bags up to her room for her. You can freshen up, Laine, then come down for dinner. I made pot roast."

Laine grinned and followed her father up the stairs. Dinner at five-thirty. Roasts on Sundays with mashed potatoes and green beans, probably from the backyard garden. A homemade pie or cake for dessert.

No wonder she'd wanted to come home. No surprises here. Nothing that could change or challenge her perceptions.

Her father deposited her bags in her room, which her mother kept exactly the way it had always been, except that she'd taken over Laine's desk to "keep herself organized."

As if she'd ever been anything but.

"Glad you're here." Her father smiled and patted her back awkwardly. Tall and wiry with large, capable hands, he looked like a farmer instead of the high school teacher he was.

"Thanks, Dad. It's good to be home." She looked around the room, taking in the flowery ruffled curtains her mom had bought over a decade ago, the walls still painted the sunny yellow shade Laine had chosen herself.

"To what do we owe the honor of this unexpected visit?"

"Oh. Well." Laine kept her gaze averted, made a random gesture as if the three-foot stuffed Dalmatian puppy at the foot of her bed provided sufficient reason. "I haven't seen you and Mom in a while, and—"

"You running away from something?"

She turned her eyes to him in amazement. Her mouth opened to contradict him, then she caught herself. Hadn't she learned anything from the situation with Grayson? She couldn't spend the rest of her life hiding or denying who she was and what she felt. If she wanted to be able to go back and make things right with him, she had to start somewhere.

"Oh, Dad. I— There's— I mean..." She squeezed frustrated hands to her temples, then let them drop. "Man trouble."

"Do I need to get out my shotgun?" He raised his bushy eyebrows, the blue eyes so much like hers, twinkling madly, sharing the joke that he wouldn't know which end of a gun to point and they both knew it.

"Nothing like that. I'm, um, apparently afraid of commitment."

There. She said it. The shameful stupid truth, generally reserved to describe immature frat boys and people with Issues, capital *I* necessary.

"Hmm. Interesting." Her father frowned toward her frog mobile hanging from the ceiling light fixture in that pensive way he had when he was preparing to dispense paternal wisdom. Wisdom that, for a change, she was dying to hear. "You know, when your sister was a child, she'd take a toy and play with it for hours. You, on the other hand, wanted a new one every five minutes."

Oh, no. A sick feeling started to party in Laine's stomach. So she'd always been like this. Unable to commit to a toy. To a course of study. To a career. To a boyfriend she loved. Even to a snack food. Ben had called her a hummingbird. Maybe he'd meant it as a compliment, but it worked the other way, too.

"But." Her dad shifted his focus back to her. "Once you found something you really liked, you stuck with it fiercely. We had to drive two hours back to our vacation hotel in Cape Cod once to retrieve Tootsie. Remember?"

Laine smiled wistfully at the threadbare stuffed dog still lying in its place of honor on her pillow. "I remember."

"You're a free spirit, Laine. But you're not a ditz. And you're not incapable of commitment. You just take time to find what you want. You tried out about a million stuffed animals before you settled on Tootsie. Applied to ten colleges before you chose Princeton, changed majors right and left, then got honors in English, graduate school in this and that, jobs here and there—it's always been that way for you. So if this guy is the right one, knowing you, there isn't a chance in hell you'll let him get away."

Tears pricked the corners of Laine's eyes. Maybe it was silly, but just hearing someone say she wasn't hopeless made her even more determined to try. "Thanks, Dad."

"You love him, I assume? Like the same things, have the same view of the world?"

"Yes." A tear spilled over. She brushed it away and smiled bravely. "It's Grayson."

"Ah." He grinned. "Still. Doesn't surprise me. Supports my theory, in fact. Always liked that one. He was too young for you in college, but then you were too young for him, too. I'm glad you found each other again."

She nodded, tears spilling over in earnest now.

Her father frowned and lifted her chin. "Did he hurt you? Is that why you came home?"

"He…" She struggled to regain control of her vocal chords. "He asked me to marry him."

Her father blinked. "This is bad?"

"I'm…not ready."

"Ah, is that all." He folded his arms across his chest, chuckling. "Your mom was skittish like that. She must have turned me down about five times."

"Really?" Laine wrinkled her nose in amazement and wiped her eyes. She had this image of her parents born already engaged, with their yard care schedule and weekly menus pinned to their diapers.

"Sure. Of course I'd only known her three days when I asked her first."

"Three days?"

He fingered his chin absently. "I think she didn't say yes until day twelve."

Laine burst into the bubbling rush of laughter that came so easily out of tears. "You call that skittish?"

"Nope." He grinned mischievously. "I call that crazy. We were both crazy. But we made it, part luck, part stubborn hard work."

Laine's laughter faded. She thought of Grayson's face when he'd given her the ring, that vulnerable hope against a backdrop of excitement, and her heart ached like crazy. "How could you be sure enough to commit after three days?"

"I couldn't, Laine. Neither can you be. Even after three years, it's always going to be part leap of faith. You can't know how the two of you will handle what life throws at you, good or bad. You just go with love and determination and a healthy dose of common sense."

"Howard." Her mother's voice rose up from downstairs. "Time to carve the roast."

He glanced at his watch, tapped it and winked devilishly at Laine. "Yes, it is."

"Oh, and tell Laine that Mimi's here."

"Okay." He winked again. "Your sister's here."

Laine laid a hand on his arm as he moved to go past her. "Are you happy with Mom?"

"Yes, I am." He nodded several times, stroking his chin. "I'd ask her all over again. Though next time I might wait longer. Maybe four days."

Laine laughed and hugged him, warmth spilling over in her chest. "Thanks, Dad."

"You'll be all right, you and Grayson. Just take the plunge. And that's my limit on fatherly advice. Your mother will have a fit if her roast isn't carved on time." He patted her cheek and went dutifully down the stairs.

Laine followed him slowly, feeling as if she was climbing down the mountain after consulting with the guru. So many years together, spent in apparent tedium, and her father would do it all again. How much had Laine missed? How many other assumptions had she jumped to without bothering to find out the truth?

"Laine!" Her sister's shriek shot Laine out of her trance and she rushed the rest of the way down to embrace her.

"Mimi, you look wonderful! Still skinny. Where are the kids?"

"Hank volunteered to watch them tonight, bless him. He knew I'd want time to see you, wasn't that sweet?" Her face glowed. "He's a doll."

"Mmm…" If Laine wasn't mistaken, the last time

Mimi mentioned Hank, she would have used another noun entirely.

Mimi laughed and squeezed her arm. "I know, I know, he wasn't a doll so much last time we spoke. Having kids can be tough. I take the strain out on him sometimes, but overall he's wonderful."

Laine nodded and hugged her sister, feeling like the one kid in the class who didn't get what everyone else understood when it was explained the first time. Mom and Dad were happy. Mimi and Hank were happy. Why hadn't she known this?

They chatted for a few more minutes, admiring clothing and hair changes until Mom summoned them to dinner, then they filed obediently into the small, crowded dining room where the table had been set with wedding china, saved only for special occasions. Mom gestured Laine and Mimi into the seats they'd occupied as girls, beaming as if she was hosting royalty.

"It is so wonderful to be a family again. I was telling Martha the other day that you two were going to be under my roof at the same time and she was just green with envy. I mean—Dad, pass the potatoes to your daughter, would you?—you'd never believe…"

The chatter flowed on, meaningless and dull, but today, like the menu and the house itself, comforting. Laine found herself joining in the conversation instead of sitting in aloof judgment, laughing at neighbor exploits, suffering over her mom's alleged decorating disasters, taking part in teasing her father for his lawn mower passion.

It was good to be home. Part of her belonged here. She'd lost sight of that for too long.

After the roast, while her mom and Mimi cleared the table for dessert, insisting Laine stay put, she tentatively tried to imagine Grayson as part of the event tonight. To her surprise, he fit right in, kicking her gently when the conversation got too gossipy, attempting to talk sports with her father who couldn't care less about them.

She tried again, a little more daring, imagining him carving a roast she'd cooked.

So far, so good.

Now tried putting that roast on the table of their home together.

Easy, Laine. Okay. She was okay.

Now, maybe a kid or two at the table?

Only a little panic. That was progress. She did the right thing coming home.

Chocolate cake was served, coffee drunk, conversation lagged with fatigue and satiation. Mom refused Mimi's and Laine's offer of help with the dishes and shooed them out to the porch for a girl chat.

"Your father and I take care of the dishes every night, we don't even think about it anymore. You two run along and talk."

They settled themselves on the new, uncomfortable plastic porch furniture, according to Mom, "on miraculous sale at Target." The sun was still fairly high in the sky, but a cooling breeze from the west helped keep the temperature comfortable.

Laine looked out at the lush green of her mother's flower and vegetable garden, her father's sacred lawn, and tried again. Thought about Grayson's house in Princeton, whether she could live there with him and commute into the city. Or whether he could move in with her. Or now that his company had Ben's account, whether they could afford to keep both places. She'd spoken to Monica before she left, and her roommate had decided to stay in Iowa permanently. So the apartment was hers—or theirs? To do with as they wished.

She smiled at her musings. Even less panic. At this rate, by morning she'd be calling *him* to propose.

At that thought, another thrill and more panic repeated their endless battle inside her.

But this time, by some incredible miracle that had happened right here in Cincinnati, Ohio, she knew which side would win.

GRAYSON PUT THE LAST of his breakfast dishes in the dishwasher and wiped down the counters. Scrubbed the sink. Then the stove.

There. Everything was clean. Ridiculously clean.

Now what?

He'd run five miles instead of two this morning; couldn't do that again. It was Saturday, he couldn't call clients. He'd done his status report, his database was up to date…

He went down the three steps into his living room, strode across it and stood looking out the sliding-glass door into the backyard, hands on his hips.

Flower beds probably needed weeding again. He glanced at the large outdoor thermometer. Sixty-five degrees. Storms last night had swept in a cooler front, thank goodness. He could turn off his A/C and open the house to some air. Then he could weed his garden.

After that…

Damn, he missed her.

The ache of loneliness and fear hadn't let up for one second, not since he'd asked her to marry him, full of confidence, and watched in this-is-happening-to-someone-else horror as she turned him down.

He moved to the thermostat next to his bookcase, snapped off the A/C and the interior fan. Went to each room, opening windows, inhaling the sweet morning breeze rushing in to replace the machine-cooled air.

He'd pressed her, of course, at least at first, until he realized it was like trying to get a response from a rock. Either she didn't know why she was resisting, or she simply wasn't telling. Either one was bad news for their relationship.

All she'd managed to stutter out was that she wasn't ready. Okay, he could live with that. But did ''not ready'' mean not now or not ever? And what was standing in the way of her readiness?

God, he was an old hen, clucking and fussing, turning the same egg over and over. But at times he was really afraid this egg had no chance of hatching into a solution.

Back downstairs, he flung open the sliding-glass door and emerged onto his brick patio, startling a blue jay who startled him right back, taking off into the air with great, angry squawks. He grabbed his weeding tool from the garage and knelt in the bed along his back fence, working methodically, front to back, right to left, pulling up miniature one-leafed sprouting oak trees, evil dandelions, the yellow-flowered, round-leafed plant they'd called ''sour grass'' as kids because of its taste.

What was she doing right now?

He'd been so sure of his goal, so sure marriage was what she wanted—the miracle cure for what ailed her.

How could he have been so stinking, drop-dead wrong? Maybe he didn't know her very well, after all. Proud and arrogant from the beginning, he'd assumed she'd fall back into bed with him, no questions asked. Assumed, once he realized he wanted more, that she would, too.

Well, he couldn't get much less proud and arrogant than he was now, trying to fill his hours, antlike, with tasks while his mind was so full of her it hurt. During this week he'd been like a robot, not even able to feel the usual supersalesman rush as Ben not only came up with project after project for Jameson Productions, but also opened doors to other hot prospects. They were set, their foreseeable future secure.

And none of it mattered next to how badly he wanted to secure a future with Laine.

What was she thinking right now?

She'd called the morning after he'd left her in a numb rage, to tell him she was going to Ohio to visit her folks, didn't know when she'd be back, but she'd call him. He didn't like the sound of that. If they had problems, he wanted her here with him so they could work them out.

In fact, on the phone with her that morning, he'd had to keep himself from saying just that. Enough trying to strong-arm her into doing what he wanted, when he wanted her to do it.

A sharp object flung down from the oak behind him and hit him on the back; a chuck-chuck-chuck scolding burst from the rustling branches over his head.

He glared up over his shoulder. Damn squirrels. Their favorite pastime was pelting him with acorns. How pathetic was this, kneeling in the dirt, bombarded by a psycho rodent, when every atom of his being screamed at him to jump on a Cincinnati-bound plane and get Laine to change her mind.

She had to change it herself. She had to want to open up to him, want to make herself that vulnerable; he'd already made it as safe as he knew how. The rest was up to her.

He finished the bed, dropped the weeds into his compost pile in the corner of the yard, replaced the tool in the garage, gave the still-chattering squirrel the finger—which instead of feeling good made him feel childish and even more ineffectual—and went back inside to his empty house, forcing himself as he'd been forcing himself all week not to think about how fabulous it had felt to have her here.

Now what?

Laundry. He could do laundry.

He took the stairs to his room two at a time, gathered laundry, picked up the basket and took it down two flights to the basement. Sorted darks and lights, added detergent, clothes, selected the proper cycle and turned the machine on.

Okay. Laundry done.

Now what?

Mow the lawn. He could mow the lawn. It had been four days, it could probably use it again.

Back upstairs, outside, opened the garage, pulled the old mower out that the house's previous owner had left, and pulled the start cord.

Nothing.

Pulled it again.

Nope.

Again.

Uh-uh.

He started to sweat, let the machine sit for a few minutes, checked the spark plug cap, the oil level, the gas level.

Tried again.

Nope.

He cursed the machine, breathing hard. Pulled the cord again. Again. Again, knowing by now he was doing more damage than good and way past caring.

Damn machine, start. *Start.*

Curses poured out of his mouth; he gave the cord one last mighty pull.

Nothing.

He clamped his hands in his hair, bent his head and stared at the moss growing between the patio bricks, trying to control his anger. Damn it, he wanted her back. Waiting around for her to find herself might be the right and honorable thing to do, but it sucked the big one. He wasn't cut out for inactivity, wasn't cut out for passive responses to big problems.

Maybe he should call Ted and talk to him, see if he knew where Grayson had gone wrong.

Except Ted had steered him most of the way into this mess.

Judy, then. Maybe she'd understand her friend better. Maybe he should call Judy and—

The absurdity of his thinking hit him in one giant sucker punch. He extracted his hands from his hair and raised his head.

There, in a squirrel's nutshell, was his problem. There was, and there always had been, only one person's advice and opinions he should be after on how to proceed.

And that person was Laine.

14

LAINE PUSHED THROUGH her building's revolving door, elated to be back east, double-elated to have the trip behind her, and triple-elated she'd soon get past the suspense over her reception from Grayson. "Hi, Roger."

The doorman's weathered face broke into an enormous grin. "Hey, welcome back, Laine, how was your trip?"

"Really nice. I hadn't been to see my parents in a long time. But it's good to be home." She smiled and nodded earnestly, knowing she wasn't going to be able to keep from asking. "Is Grayson here?"

"No." Roger fingered his large ears, an odd expression on his face. "He's been busy."

"Oh. Yes. Busy." Her elation began to deflate. What did that mean? She shifted one bag to her free hand and fidgeted with the shoulder strap of the other. "Did he say whether he'd be in the city today?"

"Not that I remember." He looked down at his desk, picked up some papers and shuffled them, as if her question made him uncomfortable.

"Oh. Okay." She fought down irrational fears. From now on she was only dealing with things she knew to be true, not things she just assumed, right? Her conversations on the phone with Grayson this week had been short and terse, full of pain, unspoken questions and all the things she wanted to say but was going to wait until they were face-to-face. "I'll come down for my mail later. Thanks, Roger."

"Okeydoke." He lifted a hand in farewell, face contorted strangely. For a weird second she thought he was trying to suppress nervous laughter.

"Are you okay?"

He looked startled at the question, flushed down to the collar on his shirt. "Never been better."

"Betty okay?"

"Fine, she's fine." He glanced at the elevator doors just opening, obviously wanting her to get on and leave him alone. What was up with that?

"Good. Tell her I said hi." She hurried into the elevator and punched number eight, pretty sure she had enough on her plate without trying to figure out Roger's problems, too. Maybe later, after she talked to Grayson.

The elevator creaked and rattled endlessly up. Laine fidgeted inside, watching the floor numbers glow in an impossibly slow procession...six... seven...eight. She burst out the doors, practically ran down the hallway, shoved her key in the lock and pushed open her apartment door. Oh, it felt good to be home. It even smelled good, not the stale air smell she expected from an apartment unoccupied for a week. Maybe Grayson had been here? Maybe he was here right now and Roger just hadn't seen him?

"Hello?" She listened, holding her breath.

The apartment answered with silence; she blew out the breath and grimaced. Silly even to hope, when Roger had been so sure Grayson wasn't around.

Her keys clattered onto the family heirloom tray;

she paused, reluctant to go farther into the empty rooms where Grayson wasn't waiting, and traced the worn silver-plated corners. It wouldn't hurt to polish the poor thing, restore some of its former luster. Maybe once she unpacked, she could—

Okay. Move, Laine. This hesitation was silly.

She stepped out of her sandals, kicked them under the hall table and turned the corner to take her bags to her room. A startled burst of laughter exited her mouth; she dropped her bags, put her hands to her face and laughed again.

A sign hanging from the kitchen ceiling in Grayson's distinctive handwriting read, Welcome Home, Laine.

And flowers. Vases and vases and vases, roses and lilies and alstromeria, asters and daisies and carnations of every color. Mixed bouquets in varying shades—blue, yellow, red, purple, magenta... On the counter, down the hallway floor. Everywhere.

"Oh." She moved forward, grinning as if she'd never be able to stop, and touched, smelled, gazed. He'd bought her flowers. Practically every bouquet in the city. He'd bought her *flowers*.

The bouquet of red roses caught her eye—a card set in the little, plastic, pronged holder poked out from among them.

She pulled it out with trembling fingers, opened the envelope and removed the card, heart pounding with hope.

I've turned into a sending-flowers kind of guy. Here are some to make up for all the ones you wanted that I never gave you.

Laine laughed again, at the same time tears welled in her eyes; she pressed the card to her heart. No wonder Roger said Grayson had been busy. Damn it, why wasn't he here?

Or maybe he was. She ran down the hall, glancing first in the room he slept in.

No.

Then to her bedroom, breathless with anticipation, imagining him lying in her bed, smiling his welcome, with only a sheet covering him…

No.

She flung herself on the bed and groaned. If he was back in Princeton she'd die of longing by the time he made it here.

She grabbed the phone and dialed his number, made a mistake, gritted her teeth and dialed again.

Ring.

Come on, Grayson, be home.

Ring.

She shifted the phone to her other ear, grabbed the scrunchy off her ponytail, tidied her hair and put it back on.

More rings. His machine picked up. Her shoulders slumped. She wanted desperately to hear his voice, to work this out, to tell him that she knew what she needed to do to make things work, that she was sorry she hurt him, that everything would be okay going forward if they could just get the chance.

The sound of a key hitting her lock turned the stab of disappointment into something else entirely. Something huge and bright and wonderful. She made a lunge for her bedroom door, turned the corner and there he was. Grayson, tall and dark and handsome and perfect in a striped shirt and khaki shorts, holding yet another vase of flowers.

She was suddenly overcome with love. And lust, oh, yes indeed, that, too.

"Hi." His voice was flat, eyes wary. "You made it back from the airport quickly."

She nodded and smiled, couldn't help it, would probably still be smiling when she died an old woman by his side. "I love my flowers, Grayson. Thank you."

He nodded and set the latest arrangement—white, cream and ivory—in an open spot. "I wanted to be here when you got back, but I had one more vase to bring up."

"It's okay." She started to close her arms over her chest and forced them to stay at her sides. "I loved walking in and seeing them."

"Good. Thanks for letting me know when you'd be back." He stood watching her, face blank, hands on his hips, legs apart in a strong stance, trying not to show his fear. Oh, she knew him so well.

"How was home? How are your parents?"

"They're fine. It was fun. Relaxing. Sanity-producing."

"Really." He looked a little hopeful on that one.

She walked toward him, fingers tangling together, stomach starting to clench. It was time. She could do this. Open her mouth and let the words she had rehearsed a million times come out. "Remember how you said you were afraid of what you felt for me? I am, too. Of what I feel for you. All the things I kept accusing you of—not opening up, not being able to commit—were my problems, too."

His face started to relax. He took a step toward her, then another, until they were nearly toe to toe. "While

I distinguished myself by consulting everyone in the universe about what you needed except you.''

She searched his gaze, saw the excitement building, knew it was mirrored in her own. ''Not that I ever volunteered that information.''

''I should have been patient and kept asking.'' His voice dropped to a whisper.

''We're such an impressive pair.''

He nodded, reached around and took out her scrunchy so her hair fell around her face, stroked it back from her cheek, hand lingering on her face. ''Very impressive in a lot of ways, Laine.''

''More than just in the bedroom.''

He nodded, his dark eyes so intense they practically went through her. ''More than just there.''

She put her hands to his chest, needing to touch his strength. The solid warmth of his muscles under the cotton nearly made her want to cry. There was so much more she wanted to say, but it stuck in her chest, a hot ball of anxiety.

He slid his arms around her waist and kissed her, slow, sweet kisses that had nothing to do with sex. She responded from the heart, willing herself to relax. She couldn't change overnight, but as long as she kept wanting to, they would only get better.

''We can talk more later. There's something else we need to do first.'' He smiled, kissed her forehead, her nose, then back to her mouth, this time lingering, letting his tongue drag along her bottom lip.

Her body took over from her heart, a humming, electric, weak-kneed response. ''You mean that thing we're so good at in the bedroom?''

''That's exactly what I mean.''

''Mmm.'' She slipped her arms around his neck.

He understood she wasn't ready for more talk now. They might not communicate everything well, but they were in tune with each other on an instinctive primal level. The rest they would learn.

Their kisses turned passionate, tongues tasting, tangling. Laine gradually let herself go, let herself get lost in the feel and love of him, felt her arousal fierce and immediate, the way it always was with him, as if she were made for him, a perfect chemical fit—and now an emotional fit, too.

He walked her backward to her bedroom, step by step, around the corner, until the bed hit the backs of her knees and she allowed herself to fall, lie there and stare up at him.

"I missed you."

"God, Laine, I missed you, too." He joined her on the bed and pulled her close. "This week was hell."

She nodded into his shirt. Hers had been good in many ways. But being held against the length of him now, in a fierce and illogical way, she missed him like crazy retroactively. "It was hell. But things will be better now."

"I can think of a way to make things *much* better now."

She giggled like a madly-in-love person. "I bet we're thinking the same thing."

"See how much we have in common?"

She giggled again, then her giggles stopped as he undressed her slowly, savoring every detail of her naked body until she was caught in a steady, strong, trancelike arousal.

They lay, skin to skin, hands and lips roaming, reexploring the curves and planes they already knew so well.

Then the sweet caresses weren't enough and Laine pulled back, reached down and took him into her hand, smooth and hard and hers. She couldn't wait to have him inside her, and it had very little to do with wanting to climax and everything to do with how she felt about him.

She stroked him lovingly, the shaft, the head, the spot he loved most at the base. His penis jumped, grew harder; she reached eagerly for a condom from her nightstand, tore open the package and rolled it over him, letting her fingers linger over his erection.

Then she lay back, parted her legs, took hold of his shoulder and urged him on top of her. This was all she wanted—him, them, slow, satisfying sex, no games, no roles. And if she disappeared into him, she'd welcome it this time, knowing it was why she'd come home to him.

He pushed inside her, said her name, gathered her close and started a slow, thrusting rhythm.

She matched him, cheek pressed to his, listening to his breathing, her eyes closed, taking in as much of the feeling and sensation of Grayson as she could, savoring the reverent silent way they were together, communicating in the way they knew best.

He pushed harder, taking their arousal up a notch. She heard the quickened pace of his breathing, felt his body begin to strain for his pleasure. Oh yes, they belonged to each other.

He lifted his head, looked into her eyes. She looked back, glancing away only once when the emotion became too intense, then made herself stay steady, showing him with her eyes what was in her heart. Why had she resisted this? The force of their joined gazes filled her, enveloped her, empowering, not threatening.

"I love you." Her mouth opened and said the words before her brain had any idea that she was going to.

"Oh, Laine." He stopped his rhythm for a second, then smiled in fierce joy. "I love you, too."

A flood of warm triumph filled her, set her completely free. She gave herself over, arms wrapped around his back and shoulders, pushing her hips against his rhythm until the wave came, the climax crashed over her, and she said his name again and again, keenly aware of his own orgasm seconds after hers started to abate.

They would make it. Forever. Love, determination and a little luck. One step at a time.

Their breaths slowed to a more normal pace; Grayson kissed her tenderly, lay with his forehead pressed to hers so their breaths mingled and she felt nearly a part of him, but this time with no fear.

"Be right back," he whispered. "Don't move."

He lifted himself off her to dispose of the condom, then lay beside her, pulled her close again, stroking up and down the curve of her waist.

"So what now, Ms. Blackwell? What do you want going forward?"

"You." She smiled, tracing the line of his lips with her pinky.

He captured her finger for a gentle bite and released it. "Done."

"But I...don't think I'm ready for marriage. Not yet."

He kissed her, a long, slow kiss that made her

throat close with emotion. "I don't know what made me think you were."

"Maybe that I wouldn't tell you what was wrong, so you had to guess." She turned and looked out the open window, at the endless blue sky, then back up at him, where her eyes belonged. "I might not always be able to tell you what I want, not right away, and sometimes I don't even know. But I'm willing to try."

He grinned. "Scarier than skydiving?"

"Yup." She nodded. "It's the same leap. Out of the airplane and hope like hell the chute holds you all the way to safety."

"I'll tell you what." He clasped her hard to him, rolled over onto his back so she was on top, and smoothed her hair away from her face. "The kind of thrills I like to chase generally involve you in the bedroom. But if you want, I'll go skydiving with you."

"You will?" She laughed and kissed his upper lip, then his lower, and both corners of his mouth. If Grayson was with her, she could do it. "So I guess this means we'll take the leap together."

He nodded, eyes dark with warmth and tenderness. "And I bet you anything our chute holds."

"Yes." Laine laughed, loving him so many times more than she had ever loved him, even though she'd loved him her whole life. "All the way to safety."

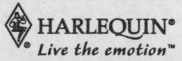

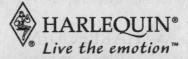

If you enjoyed what you just read,
then we've got an offer you can't resist!

Take 2 bestselling
love stories FREE!
Plus get a FREE surprise gift!

Clip this page and mail it to Harlequin Reader Service®

IN U.S.A.
3010 Walden Ave.
P.O. Box 1867
Buffalo, N.Y. 14240-1867

IN CANADA
P.O. Box 609
Fort Erie, Ontario
L2A 5X3

YES! Please send me 2 free Blaze™ novels and my free surprise gift. After receiving them, if I don't wish to receive anymore, I can return the shipping statement marked cancel. If I don't cancel, I will receive 4 brand-new novels each month, before they're available in stores! In the U.S.A., bill me at the bargain price of $3.80 plus 25¢ shipping and handling per book and applicable sales tax, if any*. In Canada, bill me at the bargain price of $4.21 plus 25¢ shipping and handling per book and applicable taxes**. That's the complete price and a savings of at least 10% off the cover prices—what a great deal! I understand that accepting the 2 free books and gift places me under no obligation ever to buy any books. I can always return a shipment and cancel at any time. Even if I never buy another book from Harlequin, the 2 free books and gift are mine to keep forever.

150 HDN DNWD
350 HDN DNWE

Name	(PLEASE PRINT)	
Address	Apt.#	
City	State/Prov.	Zip/Postal Code

 * Terms and prices subject to change without notice. Sales tax applicable in N.Y.
** Canadian residents will be charged applicable provincial taxes and GST.
   All orders subject to approval. Offer limited to one per household and not valid to
   current Blaze™ subscribers.
   ® are registered trademarks of Harlequin Enterprises Limited.

BLZ02-R

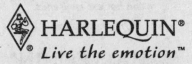

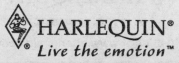